EMBER'S CROSS

A MAGICAL EQUESTRIAN NOVELLA

JOYCE BLOEMKER

LEG UP BOOK EDITING

Edited by Morgan Waddle

Print Edition ISBN: 979-8-9916113-0-5

Ebook ISBN: 979-8-9916113-1-2

First edition 2024

For Pap.

Contents

1

— • —

OCTOBER 31, 2024 7:45 A.M.

My hand hovers over the keys in the ignition. It's time to get out of the car and start the day. It's just a day with Ember, like any other. I've spent hundreds of days with her. Just because I took the day off to spend with her like I did as a teen doesn't make it any different. But my hand won't turn the key and take it out. It resists because today is supposed to be my last day with my best friend.

The car idles in front of the barn Ember's lived in for the last twenty-three years. The barn that sits on my family's old cattle farm, or what used to be a cattle farm. My family doesn't even live here anymore. My parents crossed over five years ago, leaving me alone with Ember and a 400-acre piece of land that does nothing.

Letting out a deep breath, I turn the car off and step into the crisp autumn morning. The sun below the horizon adds to the somber setting. "Thank you for Ember, and a day we will forever remember."

I sling my backpack onto my shoulder and close the car door, as a school van pulls up the driveway and Kelly and Hannah walk out of the house, their big dog, Max, following. Kelly stops on the porch before going down the steps to lift her arm to wave to me and not fall over her crutches and leg braces. Smiling, I lift my hand to wave back.

Renting out the house was the only way I could pay all the bills I inherited, and I kinda hate it. It's the house I was born in, and it's been in my family for over 200 years, but after my parents crossed, I couldn't afford to stay in it by myself. I was a senior in college with only a part-time job and a senior horse to take care of. Renting it and moving into an apartment in the middle of the small town with some college friends seemed to be my only option. *One day I'll move back in.* I hope so anyway.

The Hunters are good people, but they are different from my family. Normal.

Not witches.

At nine and twelve, Kelly and Hannah flood my mind with the memories of the fun Ember and I had at those ages. Barrel racing. Jumping. Trail riding. We did every-thing. When I was nine, Ember and I spent an entire week of our summer out in the woods making our very own cross-country course.

Dad wouldn't let me use a saw, so we rode around the woods looking for sticks and logs that weren't too big. Once we found one, I tied a rope to it, then tied the rope to Ember's saddle horn, and she dragged it back to our designated cross-country field. My grandma had taught me how to levitate things, but the logs were too heavy for me to levitate for long. Besides, Ember wanted to help.

My favorite jump was the stone wall we built. We scoured the woods looking for rocks, collecting them in Ember's saddle bags. I wanted another stone wall, but it took us most of the week to find enough stones for the one wall. Ember grazed while I piled them up, using clay I dug up from the ground to stick them together. It was my proudest achievement.

We spent hours jumping in that field over the years. I had to replace the logs once due to rotting, and although I could levitate them well by then, Ember wanted to help drag them over.

But now the old tree limbs have rotted away, turning into piles of mulch, and my stone wall has fallen down more times than I can count. We haven't jumped in years.

"Hi, Dawn!" Kelly yells as the school van drives past. I shake myself out of my thoughts. "Hi, Ember!"

The girls like to visit Ember occasionally. Sometimes she tolerates their visits, sometimes not so much.

Bang. Bang. Bang.

Ember kicks the stall door, impatiently waiting for breakfast. Well, for her this *is* patient. My lips turn up, and I walk to the barn. Last night was beautiful, so I left the barn door open for her. She loves autumn. The cool air and the crunchy leaves to play in. It's her favorite time of year.

I'm not sure I can do this. Standing at the entrance to the barn, my body has once again frozen.

The sun, just starting to creep over the horizon, pulls me to stay here and greet it. The wind makes dried leaves dance around my feet, breathing life into the world.

Inside the barn, everything is dark and still. Not even Ember is making a sound now.

Closing my eyes and taking a deep breath, I remind myself, "It's just another day with Ember."

The loss of the sunshine, what little there was, is felt immediately as I cross the threshold into the barn. A musty scent fills my nose, and the air feels damp. My eyes take a moment to adjust to the darkness before spotting Ember's red head hanging over the stall door. From the look on her face, she's getting very impatient. She'd be lifting an eyebrow at me right now if she could. The thought makes me laugh.

Ember, not finding it amusing, starts bobbing her head and kicking the stall door again.

"Okay, okay, okay. Let's feed you." I set my bag on the trunk outside her stall. "How does a maple croissant and fresh fruit sound, mad 'am?" Her snort follows me to the feed room.

The door stays locked because it's more than Ember's feed room, it's also my magic room. My collection of ingredients, spells, and tools are in here. And I don't want anyone to find them accidentally, either the Hunters exploring my home or my roommate looking for something in my room. The stories I've been told about what happens when a witch is discovered makes my skin crawl.

Most importantly in the room is my family's spell book. It's one of the oldest things I have. The pages, thin and aged, contain handwritten spells, notes, and instructions from my family past. Occasionally there's a splash of potion or a burned hole in a page. I haven't read the whole thing, it feels like every time I open it I find something new, but there are some pages that I can easily find over and over again. It's been sitting open to the pages on how to age gracefully and stop arthritis.

Glancing at it, I place two scoops of senior feed into a bucket, then I hold out my hand and twist my fingers, turning the tap on, then wave my hand towards the feed bucket to fill it with water. Rummaging through the cupboard full of my old doll house furniture for herbs, the glass jars *tink* as I shift them around looking for the stinging nettle, pumpkin, and dandelion. *This cupboard really needs cleaned and organized.* Twisting my fingers to turn off the water, I sprinkle the herbs into the feed.

With my hand open and palm down, I circle it over the feed clockwise and it all stirs together. "With this meal, help Ember heal. Increase her power over the next several hours." I close my hand, holding it over the center of the bucket. The feed bubbles with a cold boil, popping and splashing mash in the bucket. From my hand, I can see the magic of my words going into the feed. Slowly the bubbling stops and the magic has all come out of my hand.

Ember is waiting in her stall with her ears pinned, but backs so I can enter. If it was anyone else, she would not be so kind.

"A fresh breakfast for you. Would you like to eat in bed or at the table?" The old memory of making Ember have a tea party with me when I was eight brings a laugh to my lips. It didn't quite go to plan. I couldn't understand why she couldn't sit in my little plastic chair, and when she reached for a horse cookie on the table, she knocked everything off, including the tiny teacup I expected her to drink out of.

Ember nods her head and grunts. "The table it is then."
The mash slops into the corner feeder and Ember sucks it
up.

Hugging the bucket to my chest, I watch my horse enjoy her meal. Her chestnut coat used to match the bright
red of maple leaves in the autumn, but she's dulled to a
more red-brown, like old, dried autumn leaves. Leaves at
the end of autumn, signaling the start of winter. Her coat
covers her slick body. The Arabian part of her has kept
her in a slender build, but her butt is full Quarter Horse.
Big and powerful. She is built like an athlete, and we tried
every sport we wanted to. Her strong back has slowly
dipped with age, leaving a nice space to sit on bareback
but makes saddle fitting a challenge.

Ember chews and slurps up the meal, licking the feed
bucket clean. Then sneezes and looks at me.

"Ready for hay?" I rub her butt. Her slick summer coat
is starting to become thick and fuzzy for the approaching
winter. It is thick enough that I'm beginning to be able
to bury my fingers in it, my favorite part of her winter
coat.

Ember shakes her head.

"Hay time!" I double lock the stall door because Ember
has been known to be an escape artist from time to time.

Walking past Ember's lonely stall and the feed and tack
rooms, my shoulders sag as I look over the dwindling

supply of hay and I close my eyes before I can think too much. Taking a deep breath in, then slowly letting it out, my hand grasps the locket tucked safely under my shirt. Finding one of the dozen hay knifes I've lost in here, I cut the twine off a new bale. I lift my hands and a few flakes sweep into the air beside me.

Ember nickers, ears pricking forward, excited for the hay. She snags a bit as I push my hands forward and it drifts to the back corner of her stall, causing the top flake to fall on my side of the door.

"How are you going to eat it now?" Ember ignores the dropped hay and follows the hay to the corner, grinding away at the dried grasses. I lift my hands again, and the fluff of hay Ember knocked down swirls in the air and flies into the stall.

Ember raises her head suddenly and the hay rests over her ears and face like a bad wig, making me laugh. Pinning her ears, she shakes her body from head to tail, dislodging most of the hay. She is quite insulted by my laughter apparently, but I can't stop because she has just a single piece of hay sticking up between her eyes.

After entering the stall, I pick it off, smiling. "You really are a unicorn, you know that?" The piece of hay flutters from my fingers onto the pile.

The hay left in her mane and forelock is easily untangled, then I slide my hand down her red back and each leg to sweep off all the pieces of hay and stray bedding from her sleep over night.

Ember enjoys her hay, and the old broom hanging on the wall calls to me. "The barn must be swept after every feeding." That's what Gigi always said after I got Ember. "The barn may have a dirt floor, but it can still be cleaned up nicely." She said it must always be done with a broom and not magic to effectively get the negative energy out of the barn.

Starting at the hay room and sweeping out the front door, I watch the negative energy mix with the dust. Pieces of hay and dust get swirled up in the air by the stiff bristles. Close to the walls, a few fallen paint chips are added to the pile. My parents let me do anything I wanted in the barn. I lost count of how many colors I tried painting it, but nothing felt right. I wanted to have the prettiest barn. My doll houses were always the prettiest, so I couldn't figure out why the barn didn't look good. Brown was the last color I painted it, and it worked, kinda. The color looks great because it's the same as the wood it's built out of, but the paint look, looks weird. Even when I wanted to paint the barn bright pink, my parents let me and said how amazing it was.

Sweeping helps me feel lighter and freer and the barn feels warmer, more inviting, and I can't help but smile.

Full of positive energy, not negative. I twirl like a kid, more peaceful than when the morning started.

The next step of Ember's morning routine is getting her fresh water. She sometimes dunks her first bites of hay in her water, so sweeping happens first. After dumping her buckets outside, I place one under the spigot and twist my fingers to turn it on and set the other one on the ground upside down to dry. Heading to the feed room, I search for the lavender and chamomile tinctures to add to the water. The family spell book says these are the best to add to water, especially since they are already water charged by the magic of the full moon. Back outside, I twist my fingers to turn the water off and add in a few drops of each tincture.

I stir the water like I did with Ember's breakfast, then draw a five-pointed star over the surface of the water. "Give Ember peace, make the negative release. Make her feel protected, and positive energy never rejected." My fist hovers over the bucket, and the waters mix, soft yellow and purple energies swirl between my hand and the water. After waiting for the waters to fully mix and become still, I hang it back up in the stall.

Brushing is the final step of Ember's morning routine. My brushes are inside the trunk, making me have to move my bag to the ground. Ember comes over at the sound of it opening, and I fish around for a candy cane, finding some empty wrappers before I find one that's half full.

I don't know how she can tell or what the difference is, but she only likes candy canes, not peppermints. Every Christmas, my shopping cart is full of candy canes so I don't run out of her favorite treat.

Peeling the remaining candy out of the wrapper, I hold it out for Ember.

Her lips tickle my palm as she picks it up, then crunches the candy between her big teeth. Inhaling, the best smell in the world enters my nose: peppermint mixed with horse. Ember closes her eyes, too, savoring the treat.

As the peppermint scent fades, Ember shuffles back to her hay, and I pick up my curry comb and enter the stall.

2

OCTOBER 31, 2024 9:03 A.M.

The old rubber curry comb sits comfortably in my hand, and I hum. The teeth have worn down over the years, but Ember prefers it this way. Starting on her shoulder, my hand moves in slow circles, applying just enough pressure to feel like a good massage.

Ember isn't dirty, I brushed her last night when she ate dinner, so not much dust is floating off her. She enjoys the massage and humming though. As my hand moves from her back to her stomach, she stops chewing and closes her eyes. My humming always puts her in a calm trance.

We both let out a sigh at the same time, relaxing into our familiar routine. Switching the curry comb from one hand to the other, I curry her other side. Her long mane falls to this side, so I push it over the top of her neck.

Her itchy spot is at her withers, and she leans into the curry comb when it passes over it.

The familiar motion of currying Ember, the soft smells of hay and horse, the sound of hay under my feet, and my humming helps me fall into a relaxed state. My focus solely on currying Ember's back, belly, and rump.

Once she's all curried, I grab my dandy brush to flick the dirt off in quick flips of my wrist while still humming. This process isn't exactly the most relaxing, but I try my best to keep a rhythm to my flicks. It's over quickly and my favorite part of the grooming process can begin: the soft brush.

The soft brush can be done in long, slow movements. From the base of her ears, down her mane line to her shoulder, the brush glides. Then it follows the same path, just a few inches below until it brushes the bottom of her neck. Putting the brush back under her ear, I brush her entire neck again, just to make sure she's completely clean and shiny. Humming, I work my way to her shoulder, down her leg, to her back and belly, to her rump and hind leg before doing it all again on the other side. Long, fluid strokes cover every inch of her body.

Last to be brushed is her face. The small, soft face brush glides around her ears, eyes, and nose, following the growth pattern of the hair. Leaning in, I give her white crescent moon marking on her forehead a kiss.

Finally, I comb out her mane, tail, and forelock with my fingers until they are smooth as silk, putting the hairs that come out in my jean's pocket. My fingers carefully untangle any knots they come across, and they comb through the same section a few times, just to make sure no pesky knots are left.

My fingers run through her silky tail and I look her over. Her coat doesn't shine like it used to, but it's the best I can do. Ember stands with her eyes half closed, her ears and lower lip dropping, and her hind leg cocked. *If only she could stay like this forever.*

My feet shuffle back to her face while my hand slides across her back. Standing for a moment, I place my hands on her neck behind her ears, close my eyes, and take a deep breath. The hum changes and my hands slowly move from the top of her head, down her back, over her rump, up and down her legs, and over her face, making a big circle over her.

Although my eyes can be open, I like to do this with them shut. The energy is louder with them shut.

My dad showed me this healing energy technique when Ember turned eighteen while my mom sat on the trunk watching. Healing magic was his specialty.

My hands run over Ember's body slowly, pausing at any points where her energy feels off. Some spots have been around for years and just never really go away, and some spots come and go. There aren't too many extra points today, and the regular ones feel like they typically do. Over those spots, my hands pause, and I breathe deeply. "Let my touch heal Ember much. Energy do your mending so she lives never-ending." Heat comes into my palms, taken from the energy in the air, and travels from them into Ember's body. The amount of heat for each spot is different. Her joints, which have been regular spots for a long time, always take the longest and have the most heat.

This healing energy process can take a long time to do, depending on how she's feeling. Days when I don't have a lot of extra time with her, which are rare, I send her full body healing.

Once the healing magic has touched every part of Ember, she stands relaxed, so I grab some massage oil from the feed room. The peppermint oil permeates the air as I massage it into her neck and back before rubbing the lavender into her legs, still humming.

Between the herbs, spells, healing energy, and massage with natural oils, she should feel great for a long time. My hands drop and my humming stumbles. *But she's not.*

I have done everything the spell book and my dad have told me to do to help her age, but it hasn't been enough. *Why hasn't it been enough?* She's only twenty-seven. Horses can live to be in their thirties, even forties. She's still young.

My hands go back to massaging Ember's joints, a voice popping up in the back of my head *"Today is Ember's last day"* but I ignore it. Push it away.

With Ember's autumn shots, the vet did a full lameness exam. He said she was doing pretty good for her age. *Then why does today have to be her last day?*

"I'm tired. It's time." That's the message Ember has been giving off for the last month. Sometimes it's so faint I pretend like I don't hear it. Other times it's a yell, but I still pretend I don't hear it. The message makes my stomach drop each time.

Massaging lavender into her last joint, there's nothing left I can think to do, so I finish and exit the stall, grabbing my water bottle and taking a big drink. My hands are covered in a few layers of dirt while the rest of my body is covered in dirt, hay, sweat, and even some of Ember's breakfast. I look the total opposite of my horse. Shrugging my shoulders, I gulp down half my water. It's impossible to stay clean in the barn. I gave up trying years ago.

Growing up, even when I would just feed Ember and come right back to the house, I'd have at least one piece of clothing covered in a mysterious stain or goop, and my mom would make me change. Three or four outfits in a day was normal for me. I swear I would try so hard to stay clean, but the more I tried, the dirtier I got, so I gave up. Sometimes I made it a game to get as dirty as I could.

My parents laughed and enjoyed the game, too, even if it meant occasionally showering a couple of times a day. No matter how dirty I was, my parents never yelled or got mad. They just asked me to strip down on the porch and go right to the bathroom to clean up.

Ember yawns and arches her neck and back, coming out of her trance. After I set my water down, I follow her lead and stretch. I've never spent quite so long brushing her before and I didn't realize how stiff my back got doing it. She looks amazing though. Ready for a show. Blinking, she looks at me with love in her eyes.

"What next, girl? Do you actually want to eat your hay or–" Ember's head reaches over the stall door, nudging me in the chest. "Alright," I laugh. "Shall we go for a little ride?"

I put my bag back on top of the trunk, reaching inside but hesitate. Ember nods, so I pull out my good camera from my backpack.

3

——— • ———

OCTOBER 31, 2024 11:48 A.M.

"Smile." I start snapping pictures of Ember's head over the stall door. She arches her neck and pricks her ears, posing for a few pictures before she flicks her tail, letting me know she's ready to head out.

Placing the camera back on the trunk, I go to the tack room to grab my Western saddle and pad. The green wool pad sails onto her back with ease, and the heavy saddle makes me grunt as I swing it up, trying to place it gently on her back before slowly doing up the cinch.

In the tack room, I study my two breast collar and bridle sets. One set is plain and worn. I've used it since I started riding Ember Western. My eyes flick from it to my English tack sitting under a layer of dust. I love riding English, but she hasn't jumped for years. At nineteen, the vet said no more jumping or high levels of exercise. She got a tendon injury in her front right leg, and although it was minor and healed well, the vet suggested she retire from hard work. Trail riding is kinda all she can do now, and Ember seems to prefer the Western saddle for trails.

We did so much in that English saddle. Jumping was one of my favorite activities with Ember, even if she loved the trails more. That's why we built a cross-country course. It was a way to combine our favorite things.

We loved going to occasional shows. Jumpers was our best English event. Ember may not have always been the prettiest to jump, but she did like going fast. Which is why we started doing barrel racing and pole bending.

My eyes find the new breast collar and bridle set. The swirls carved into the leather are painted red, orange, and yellow to look like flames. I bought it for myself as a birthday present four years ago, after my parents crossed over because there wasn't anyone else to buy me a present. I've regretted spending the money on it ever since. I really couldn't–and still can't–afford to spend money on something so frivolous, but I didn't have the heart to take it back either. It's just so beautiful. I've only used it for special rides, which isn't often.

My cheeks fill with air and it comes out in a fast and frustrated puff. *It shouldn't take me five minutes to pick up a bridle.*

My hand snatches up the flame set and my feet march back out to Ember, pausing in the doorway. Studying the flame set in my hand, my lips fall to a frown. *I don't want this to be a special ride.*

Ember bobs her head and kicks her stall, impatiently waiting for me to let her out.

Hanging the bridle on the hook on the stall door, I step inside to attach the breast collar to the saddle. Ember stands, but her feet move in anticipation of leaving. The bridle slips over her ears and rests on her head. A perfect fit.

Ember looks beautiful in the tack set. She used to match the reds and oranges painted onto the leather. But with her duller coat, the painted colors really pop. I quickly braid back my long hair before leading her out of the barn, picking up the camera and my helmet from the trunk on the way.

We pause in the sunshine, letting our eyes adjust to the light and enjoy the warmth of the sun on our faces.

With my spirits slightly lifted, I snap more pictures of Ember from every angle, but she's eager to hit the trails and doesn't stand for too long. She moves stiff coming out of the barn, so I lead her for a bit to warm up.

"Where should we go first?" I pat Ember. She walks to the right, towards the biggest section of woods on the property. There are patches of woods and open pastures all over the farm, and to the left is an open pasture with a pond in it. The thought of the pond sends a shiver down my spine. It's the last place I want to be today, especially since it's the start of the ride tonight. The midnight ride on All Hallows' Eve is one of the best rides of the year, but tonight I want to hold it off as long as possible.

To help loosen her up, I chant, "Walk away her aches and pains, and send youth down her veins."

Ember marches into the woods, away from the pond, and I occasionally snap pictures of her, stopping in the occasional leaf pile to get a good picture, lifting my hands to make the leaves dance around her.

"Good thing I cleared the memory card last night. It'll be full before lunch!" I study the last photo. *Perfect.* Then glance at my watch and see lunchtime is not that far away after all. *Today is fading away.*

About half a mile down the trail, Ember walks much easier. The cinch is tight, and the camera strap is around my body, securing the camera. Ember stands beside a tree stump, and I swing up onto her back.

We mosey along the trails we helped create years ago with my parents. Some were there from the years of cattle on the farm, but we also made some of our own. My parents didn't ride, but we loved to hike and explore the farm whenever we could. There are buildings all over the property, some easily accessed and some not, that we explored. They were all once used for one purpose or another but are all abandoned now. Some of the buildings around the house and barn we still used, like the wood-working and blacksmith sheds. When I was little, my parents would hike or bike along the trails with me and Ember. Once I started galloping away from them, they would let me go out on my own, but with a walkie-talkie to keep in contact. The days before cell phones were great.

Sometimes in the summer, my parents and I would pack up supplies, hike around the farm and spend a couple of nights camping as we explored new parts we hadn't seen before.

A few times a year, we would go around the farm and harvest different herbs, flowers, and other plants to use for spells. They taught me how to identify every plant on the farm and know what magic it could help with.

There are miles and miles of trails. Ember and I could never ride them all in one day, even if we wanted to, and we've tried. Plus, I haven't been able to take care of them all anymore, but I clear the ones Ember loves every spring. The trail to the cross-country course is one I always clear, and it's the one we're on now.

Ember perks up to a trot when the fallen leaves on the path grow thick, and I can't help but laugh at her playfulness and enjoyment. No one sees the beauty in autumn leaves like Ember. I lift my hands, piling leaves up along the trail for her to trot through. She picks her feet up and dances through the leaves. My heart warms at her love of autumn, and I take more pictures of Ember from her back.

The trees on our right start to thin out, letting us know we are almost to our cross-country course. I press with my left leg to move her over so I can get a good look at it when we pass. She starts to snort and toss her head, realizing we're almost at our old course. "We had fun here, didn't we?"

The last tree is past us, and Ember turns into the field that's opened up by herself, and my heart sinks. Our course does not look good. None of the logs are logs anymore. The stone wall is just a pile of rocks, and big, ugly weeds have taken the grass in the clearing over. *Is this what it looked like in the spring?* This isn't how I want to remember our course.

Ember doesn't seem bothered by it. She's hopping in place, wanting to move faster. Letting her follow the tree line around the clearing, she picks up a choppy canter, which lifts my heart. Cantering has been a struggle for Ember for a while now.

One choppy lap around the cross-country field uses up Ember's energy. And we walk back out onto the trail and head for the creek that's not too far away.

The creek is our favorite spot for a break. I dismount so Ember can have a drink, rest, and quick snack. While I snap even more photos of her, I wade across the creek and only once does my warn boot slip into the water, getting my foot wet from the hole in my once waterproof shoes.

Ember snags a few bites of grass but prefers to doze off. A big flat rock on the bank of the creek is my sitting spot. My shoes are off to dry my foot and my knees are hugged up to my chest. My chin rests on my knees as I sit watching Ember. *I could stay like this forever.*

Two deer come running up to the creek from the other side, only noticing Ember and me as they slow down. Their eyes bug out, not sure what to do about us. Turning around, they run back from where they came. I smile at Ember, sleeping through the whole thing.

A tree branch snaps, and the sound of it and the leaves falling on the ground behind me finally wakes her up. Amazingly, she's unbothered by it, looking at me with a "why did you wake me up?" look on her face.

"Good nap?" I slip my feet back into my shoes, not really any dryer than before. "I think it's time to head home."

I tighten her cinch and bring her over to the rock so I can mount.

We're about half a mile from home on another trail when Ember spooks at a turkey in the tree branches above us and stumbles over a pile of leaves. Being thrown forward, I instinctively reach for the camera hanging on my side while Ember stops and throws her head up, hitting my head on her raised neck.

"What's wrong?" I rub my nose.

My legs squeeze her sides, but Ember stays still as a statue. My legs squeeze harder and click to her, asking for a walk, but she won't move. Frowning, I dismount. "What happened?" I try to move her forward, but she won't budge, and the blood drains from my face.

This can't be happening. Not now.

I clutch my locket.

She has to make it till tonight. At least.

Why did I take her out for a ride? How stupid can I be? Eleven hours. That's how much longer I needed to keep her safe and I went and ruined it!

I run my hands down each of Ember's delicate legs. They're damp and muddy, but there's no swelling or heat to indicate a problem.

"Nothing seems to be wrong. Can you walk?" I try again to get her to walk. She resists until I'm at the end of the reins, pulling gently on her face before she finally takes a step. Limping, she throws her head high with the step.

I run my hands down her lame leg. I don't feel anything off, but send as much healing energy as I can. "Mystery pain go away, let Ember move like she's in a ballet."

Tears burn my eyes as I run my hand down the lame leg again and still feel nothing. "Can you make it home?" Ember nods but keeps her eyes forward. She won't look at me.

Very, very slowly Ember limps her way back to the barn. I cry silently whispering, "Take away the lame, make Ember's legs all feel the same," and sending her healing energy the whole way.

4

OCTOBER 31, 2024 2:39 P.M.

Once we reach the barn, my tears have dried, and my mind is clear. Standing outside the stall, I run my hand down the lame leg again to still find no heat or swelling. There's only one other thing that could cause the sudden lameness, which I can't believe I didn't think of before.

My hoof pick is buried in my trunk. Even with a full barn, tack room, and feed room, my trunk is full of the most random, sometimes useless things. Empty candy cane wrappers, a lead rope, twine, and some doll house furniture. The hoof pick, stuck inside a doll toilet, puts up a fight to come loose.

Ember easily lifts the lame leg, and sure enough, there's a pointy rock poking into the bottom of her hoof. I remove it and ask Ember to walk forward. Her walk is easy, willing, and without a limp.

"Thank you, thank you, thank you," I sigh while closing my eyes. My hand runs down each leg, pick ready to do its job. Holding her legs up can be challenging for Ember sometimes now, so I don't always clean them. The pick scrapes off clumps of mud from her feet, but no more stones. My back spasms as I try to stand up straight from the last hoof. The only movement Ember makes is flicking her ears back at my slight groan. A few steps loosen my back enough for it to straighten out again.

The bridle gently slips off Ember's head, and the old, green halter that was hanging on the stall door feels soft against my fingers as it replaces the bridle on Ember's head. The halter is no longer pretty, but it's the first one I ever bought for Ember. It was once a bright hunter green with shiny metal pieces, but the metal has rusted, and the color has almost completely faded away. It's tattered and well-worn. The rusted clip refuses to open wide enough to let the ring slip inside, but it finally allows it with a chunk of something brown falling to the ground.

I use the matching lead rope, not quite as faded, to tie Ember to the loop outside her stall.

Soft leather of the cinch easily releases its knot, and the saddle slides off her back. I replace the tack to its spots in the tack room, leaving it all to be cleaned another day.

From the trunk, I pull out the dandy brush to sweep over her body again. The hairs that were under her saddle and cinch are pressed down, but no sweat marks are visible. She stands, her eyes closed and hind leg cocked. I hum, slowly sweeping the brush in long strokes along her back.

Moving around her body slowly with the brush, her coat fluffs up again. It doesn't take long to finish brushing her this time, and when it's over, she gives a big yawn, rolling her eyes into the back of her head. She shakes, causing the loop to clang against the wall. I reach up and untie the lead rope. "Come on, let's go outside."

She follows me around the barn to the small pasture in the back. A dirt path has formed from our walking the same path from the barn to the pasture over the years. The gate swings open as we walk inside, and I take off Ember's halter. "Go. Graze. I'll be right back." I wave my hand vaguely to the back of the pasture, close the gate behind me, and hang the halter on one of the posts.

She's standing there, head high, eyes on me, and ears pricked. "Go!" I laugh, turning back to the barn. Peaking over my shoulder reveals Ember still standing at the gate watching me.

Shaking my head and smiling, I go back into the barn. A paper bag sits on the ground beside my backpack with my name on it. *Was this here when we got back?* Inside is a pepperoni roll, a bag of chips, and two apples. There's also a thermos of tea beside it.

Clearly Mrs. Hunter was here. She's very motherly, often inviting me to dinner, at least once a month. After about six months or so of declining, she insists I can't say no. The dinners are delicious, the best meals I've ever eaten, but it's weird sitting in my family home with another family.

Grabbing the camera, I take the lunch back out to the pasture. Ember is grazing in the middle of the pasture now and lifts her head as I open the gate. The big tree standing by itself towards the back of the pasture is where I sit. Under it, I set down my lunch, keeping my camera in hand. Ember grazes, lifting her head to pose occasionally for me. The camera captures Ember from every angle. She wanders over to the small cluster of trees surrounding the side of the fence that, if framed just right, looks like she's in the woods. I twist my wrist and the leaves swirl, creating a perfect circle around her. Adjusting my hands just right, the leaves dance into different patterns.

With a pin of her ears and a sneeze, Ember wanders to the big tree. My hands lower as she sniffs my lunch. "Get out of there. Get." I shoo her away. She snorts and trots behind the tree. The bag crinkles as I take the pepperoni roll out of it. Wrapped in foil, I peel the wrapper open and smell the heat escaping. The warmth quickly evaporates into the air, but I don't move.

Ember comes around the other side of the tree and picks at the limited grass between the roots. My hand grasps my locket, playing with it. I nibble at my lunch. Inch by inch, Ember gravitates to my side and sniffs the partially eaten pepperoni roll. Smiling, I re-wrap it and put it back in the bag, taking out an apple. It crunches between my teeth, juice dribbling down my chin. Ember bobs her head. I hold my hand out flat with the apple on it. She grabs the apple in one bite, chewing, slurping, and dribbling on my feet. "Gross!" An apple piece falls onto my boot. Ember lips it back up.

Sighing, I take out the other apple and bite into it. It's just as crunchy and juicy as the first. Ember's nose is immediately in my face. "Chew," I tell her, my own mouth full of apple. Only getting another bite out of the apple for myself, Ember is about to step on me, so I toss the apple a few feet in front of me. She follows it, taking it in one bite, dirt and all.

A leaf falls, landing on the thermos beside me. Feeling bloated and nauseous, the warm ginger tea soothes my stomach.

Ember, having finished her apple, grazes on the good grass in the middle of the pasture. Sipping the tea, my hand scans the ground for something to fiddle with. Dirt, roots, leaves, and acorns brush against my fingers, but none of them feel right. My hand lands on two twigs, causing me to set the tea down to pick them up. Without looking at them, I pick a long piece of grass and start twisting them around together, humming. I look down to pick up my tea, but stop. The twigs are tied in the shape of a cross. I throw it and Ember lifts her head as I stand suddenly.

Moving to the middle of the pasture, where there are fewer leaves, I lay on the cool ground. The air has a cool bite to it, but the sun's rays provide warmth. The sunlight sinks into my body as I stretch over the ground, warming me in the brisk afternoon. Leaves are crunching under every move I make, tickling my neck. There is not a comfortable spot to be found, so I move my arms and legs, attempting to make a leaf angel, then laugh at myself. *I haven't done this in years.*

My parents and I would come to this pasture in the autumn and rake big piles of leaves for Ember to jump into and run through. We loved watching her play in the leaves. Eventually she would get down and roll, and one year I decided to try to make a leaf angel. They aren't quite as good as snow angels, but Ember enjoys them a lot more.

Ember grunts, causing me to bolt up. Her legs kick in the air, scratching her back against the ground. She picked a place closer to the tree, so she's crunching a lot of leaves while grunting and groaning as she heaves her big body side to side over them. I flick my wrist and send leaves to pile up under her to add to her enjoyment, then lay on my side, resting my head on my hand, watching Ember, and smiling. There is not a word to describe her love and joy of rolling around in them. She gets so excited when she first sees a leaf on the ground in the autumn. She leaps on it to crunch it like a cat pouncing on a mouse, and I never get tired of watching it.

She finishes rolling and looks at me.

"Nothing beats a good roll, huh, girl?"

Ember nods her head, then rests it down on the ground.

I sit up for a moment, worried, but Ember sighs, resting her chin on the ground to take a nap.

Ember can find so much joy in just the simplest of things. An autumn leaf. A good scratch. *How can she find so much good in the world?*

Laying there watching her nod in and out of sleep for half an hour is peaceful until the cool ground has sucked my body heat from me. Ember lifts her head at my standing and nickers softly.

"What?" I whisper, slowly approaching her. She touch-es my outstretched hand with her nose then nods towards her shoulder.

What is she doing?

She does the movement again, touching my hand then nodding to her shoulder.

"Do you want me to sit here?" She's let me come up to her while laying down before, but she's never let me sit with her. I cautiously lower myself to the ground and cuddle into Ember's side. She watches me settle in, then rests her head and closes her eyes again.

I comb her mane with my fingers, saving the stray hairs that come out in my hand. Slowly relaxing more and more, I melt into Ember's chest and neck, her big body enveloping me with warmth.

5

— · —

OCTOBER 31, 2024 4:26 P.M.

I blink my eyes open, stretch my arms out, and look around. Jumping slightly at the sight of Ember's head right beside me, I calm at Ember's gentle eyes watching me.

"Well, good afternoon," I yawn. Stretching, I push myself up on stiff legs. My body aches less than it did after brushing Ember, and I reach my hands up and arch my back. My palm tickles, and in it is Ember's mane hair. I add it to the rest in my pocket.

Stepping to the side, I give Ember the room to stretch out and roll again. She grunts, rubbing her neck against the ground, then staggers to her feet. Lowering her head, she arches her back and yawns. Then starting with her head and slowly incorporating every part of her body, she shakes so violently she knocks herself off balance.

She circles around with her nose on the ground, looking for some good grass. The side she was lying on is covered in dirt, leaves, and even a few sticks. "Now I need to groom you again." She looks back at me, probably wanting to roll her eyes, and shakes her whole body again, but not quite as hard. The second shake doesn't dislodge any of the dirt.

Under the tree, I pick up the camera and turn to look at Ember and pause. Shaking my head, I pick up the lunch bag and walk to the gate, kicking at the leaves when my toe catches on something. The cross I made is under my foot. Frowning at it, I'm about to kick it across the field when Ember comes up behind me and her nose tickles the back of my neck.

"This is important."

Sighing, I pick it up and carry it back to the barn.

Setting the cross down, I chug the last of my water before grabbing the dandy brush and heading back outside. Ember waits at the gate. With a light press against her chest, she backs up so I can open the gate to get in. She sniffs the brush in my hand, checking for any food, and finding none, she turns to place her dirty side in front of me.

After I'm done, she trots away and canters a few laps around the field, even throwing in a small buck. I laugh at her playfulness and joy at being alive. Stopping behind the big tree, Ember pokes her head between the branches. I run over and press my back against the trunk. She walks around the tree, ears pricked, and startles when she spots me, then ducks and trots away and I chase her.

I wish I had the camera to capture this!

We chase each other around the tree, and I laugh. We play until we're out of breath and we mosey to the gate together, my hand resting on her back. I grab the halter off the post and slip it back on her head. I have no idea what time it is, but it must be getting close to her dinner time.

The Hunters make their way over to us as we walk out of the gate.

"Be good," I whisper to Ember.

"Hi, Dawn! Hi, Ember!" Kelly calls. "We're going to Ruby's to trick-or-treat. Can we take a picture with Ember? I brought some candy for her too."

Both girls are dressed in bright, sparkly outfits. Even their parents have on some costumes, minimal but fun.

"That sounds like fun," I say. "One of the bad things about living out on the farm is no trick-or-treating."

"Oh, it's okay. Ruby lives in a HUGE neighborhood. We'll get so much candy. Especially with my crutches and her wheelchair."

"Kelly!" her parents scold her. Hannah rolls her eyes under thick, fake eyelashes.

"It's true…" Kelly shrugs her shoulders. "Well, can we get a picture with Ember?"

Sharing a smile with Mr. and Mrs. Hunter, I say, "Ember seems to be very calm today. I think you can get a nice photo with her. She's nice and clean too."

"Yay!" Kelly cheers. "I'm a mermaid and Hannah is a witch." Kelly nods to her sister. "Have you ever dressed up as a witch for Halloween?"

"Wonderful costumes." Their costumes are almost cartoonish. No one in my family has ever dressed like Hannah. No black dress, pointy hat, and definitely no green skin! But that's what trick-or-treating is for, I guess. Dressing boldly and having fun. They both hold out the back of their hands to Ember like I've shown them: the horseman handshake. "No. I've never been trick-or-treating."

"Never?" Kelly's mouth hangs open.

"No, my family has always had a small gathering on Halloween night."

"Couldn't you get out of it? Just once?"

"No, it's a family tradition."

"Let's take the photo," Mr. Hunter says.

I hand the lead rope to Hannah, who smiles and quietly thanks me, and step aside to let Mr. Hunter snap a few photos. His pumpkin hat matches his shirt that says "This IS my costume." It makes me chuckle.

"Thank you," Mrs. Hunter whispers, handing me a box of candy canes. Her smile matches her costume of a black shirt with a red and white polka dot skirt and mouse ears on a headband. "I know it's not an easy day for you, but Kelly really wanted to show Ember her costume. And she begged and begged us to order some candy canes to give her for Halloween. Sometimes it's just so hard to say 'no' to her. I figured Ember would really appreciate them this year." She holds out a thermos and a spoon. "Here's some chili to keep you warm tonight. It shouldn't be too bad, but being outside all day in the autumn always leaves a chill in my bones." She gives a little shiver.

Smiling, I fight down the tears spiking in my eyes. "Thank you. Ember will love them. And it's okay. It's nice to have their smiles around, and Ember is in a good mood today." Ember hugs the girls into her side with her head, making us all laugh and doesn't even react to the sparkles that would have normally spooked her. She's extra sweet and gentle with the girls.

"Max is already locked in the basement," Mrs. Hunter continues. He loves me but hates anyone outside at night. I try my best not to come to the farm after dark, but this is the one night a year it can't be helped. Ever since I started riding Ember, I've spent the night of All Hallows' Eve riding with Gigi.

"Thank you. I really appreciate it." I grab my locket. Mrs. Hunter's eyes flicker to it, and I let it go.

"Of course. It should be a nice night for a ride." Mrs. Hunter looks up to the sky, the sun lowering with not a cloud to be seen. She looks back to me and pulls me into a side hug. "Okay girls, we have to go or we'll be late."

"Bye, Ember." Kelly pets her shoulder and walks to me. "Thanks, Dawn. Here." She hands me a seashell covered in glitter. "This is for Ember. It has mermaid magic in it to make her feel young again, like you always say you want her to feel. Happy Halloween! Oh, and could you help me redecorate my room? I want it to be mermaid themed." She swivels her hips, and her tail skirt shimmies around her legs.

The shell in my hand is damp with glue. "Of course I can help you with your room."

"Thanks, Dawn," Hannah says quietly, handing the lead rope back to me. For once her long dark hair isn't hanging in her face.

"You're welcome, girls. Happy Halloween." I try to smile, but my eyes sting with tears and I turn around to walk back to the barn so they don't see me crying.

In her stall, Ember takes a nice big drink of water before turning, her lips dribbling, to the hay she abandoned this morning.

I take the box of candy canes to the feed room and mix up her evening feed, the same thing as this morning, but with all the candy canes crushed and mixed in. I add my magic to it, then take it back to the stall.

Ember politely waits for her meal. Then eats slowly, savoring every bite.

I look around the stall when she's done. "You really do know how to make a mess in here," I tell her.

Manure is all over the stall. She used hay from her dinner last night to make a bed, and the fluff of hay that landed on her head this morning is in a big pile in the corner. Tears sting my eyes. "I'll do it later. No point in wasting time on that tonight."

Not when we have so little time left.

6

OCTOBER 31, 2024 5:37 P.M.

Ember munches on fresh hay, and I sit with her in the stall. The cross sits on the floor, and I pick it up to play with it some more. Spinning it around and looking at it from every angle, my eyes narrow. *It's missing something.* I pull the hairs out of my pocket, braid some together, then tie the braid around the center of the cross. It looks much better now, but *too* good and I hate it again. Sensing my hatred, Ember looks over her shoulder at me. Sighing, I stand up and put it on the trunk and check my phone. There is only one missed text from Mrs. Hunter, asking if they could come over in their costumes.

I check the time, 5:54, and look outside.

"The sun is setting, want to go watch it?" I ask in a quiet voice. Ember lifts her head from the hay and meets me at the stall door. After slipping her halter back on, we go back out to the small pasture and watch the sunset. Well, Ember watches it. I watch Ember. She's beautiful in the changing light, and she keeps her eyes on the sky. *Does she watch the sun set regularly?* As the sun turns the entire sky red, Ember's coat shines brightly like it once did. I want to take some pictures of her, but the camera is in the barn and I just can't leave her.

I look at my watch. 6:32.

In the darkness, Ember grazes again, using her powerful lips to find the best grasses, and I sit under the tree, pulling my flannel shirt tight around me as the air quickly cools down. The Hunters drive up the driveway and I wave. The headlights don't let me see them, but I'm sure if Kelly or Mrs. Hunter saw me sitting here, they would be waving.

The cold sinks into my bones, and Ember comes over to me, blowing her hot breath into my face. "Want to go back inside?"

Leading Ember into her stall, I spot the thermos of chili. Even though I haven't eaten much of anything today, the thought of food makes my stomach twist in knots and my throat close up.

Only closing the stall door and not locking it, I search in my backpack for the sweatshirt I packed. It's pretty big for me since it was my dad's. A gray sweatshirt that says "Steelers" across the front. It was one of his favorites, not one he would ever wear into the barn. The anger I feel towards my parents for crossing without even telling me is not fully outweighed by my love for them. I had the best childhood and best parents. *Why did they leave me like they did? What did I do to upset them so much?*

Pulling back the bulky sleeve, I look at my watch: 6:51.

Ember dozes in the stall, and I join her. Wanting to do something, think about something, I run my hands over her body, sending healing energy and extra love to any spot that feels off.

Too quickly I'm done. There weren't too many spots that needed healing, and they can only take so much in one day. Ember's breath is slow and regular as she naps, and I head to the feed room and open the family book to the page marked with the black ribbon.

This spell isn't used very often, so the pages aren't as worn. It's a complicated spell with many ingredients. I read the list carefully and gather everything it says is needed, including candles, a satchel, and crystals. Thinking I have everything, I put the ingredients and the book into my backpack.

Checking the time, 7:13, I'm not sure what to do next. Looking around, I see the mess from picking out Ember's feet in the aisle. It doesn't need to be cleaned up tonight, but Ember's still sleeping. My hands and legs start twitching because I'm standing still. Grabbing the broom, I sweep the barn again. It wasn't dirty this morning and only the hoof cleanings have made it dirty now, so sweeping doesn't take nearly as long as I want it to.

7:24.

Up and awake, Ember munches on her hay. Sitting in her stall, I'm exhausted, but my eyes stay open, glued to her. Occasionally they slip down to my watch.

7:46.

8:01.

8:22.

I can't stop looking at my watch, the minutes ticking by so fast.

8:36.

My hands shake as the night progresses. Ember pins her ears and swishes her tail at me, my nervous energy disturbing her. This should be a good night. We should want to spend every moment cuddled together. But my nerves won't calm down, so Ember won't come over to me.

8:52.

Standing, I try approaching her, but she turns her butt to me, preventing me from getting too close. "Can't we just be together?" My voice shakes and she stomps her hind foot. I get the message.

"Not while you're so nervous."

I lock her in her stall and gather a dozen jars from the feed room. I might as well prepare water to be charged by the full moon tonight since Ember doesn't seem to want me around. Filling them with water, I add lavender to some, chamomile to others, rose to another, and leave the rest as they are. Carrying them outside two at a time, I set them on the old bench leaning against the front of the barn. I leave the lids inside so the water can get as much moon magic as possible.

Once done, my body wants to keep moving, but my mind only wants to be with Ember. I go back to her stall, forcing myself to sit still with her.

9:09.

My body is stiff, it can't stand not moving anymore. I have to stand to stretch, and I take the opportunity to run my hands down Ember again, sending her healing energy. She's never had this much healing in one day. No spots feel like they really need or can take any more, but I just don't know what else to do. She swishes her tail at me but lets me work on her.

9:22.

It's getting closer and closer to midnight. Less than three hours away from losing my best friend, my only family member. My body shakes uncontrollably.

9:46.

Ember calmly eats her hay. *How can she be so calm? Why is she ignoring me? Do I mean nothing to her?* I grab the locket. *Doesn't* this *mean anything to her anymore?*

When I first made it, she was so excited to check it out. She sniffed it all over with both nostrils and lipped at it, never biting down. For the next two months, she always had to sniff it when I came to visit. Her ears and eyes perked up in excitement over it. She still did it occasionally, always happy about it, but she didn't acknowledge it today. *Why didn't she sniff it today?*

10:01.

I sit on my hands because they won't stop shaking and to try to calm myself.

10:16.

Why won't time just stop?

10:22.

It just keeps going faster and faster.

10:29.

The clock keeps ticking closer and closer to the start of our yearly ride.

10:34.

My body refuses to sit still. I stand. Ember pins her ears at me again but walks over. She puts her head on my shoulder, trying to comfort me, and I hug her.

10:38.

Lifting her head off me, I back away, step out of the stall, and pace. Ember looks over the stall door, watching me go up and down the aisle. Calmness in her eyes. *How is she so calm?*

10:45.

I grab the broom to try to sweep the barn again, but my hands are shaking so badly I break off the bristles instead of sweeping. So I set it down.

10:48.

Pacing again, my hand clenches at the locket beneath my shirt. Ember keeps her eyes on me. She's relaxed. *How can she be relaxed?*

10:52

I can't take it anymore. Ember is fine. She will be fine. Nothing will happen to her tonight. I'll make sure of that.

"See you tomorrow, girl." I stuff everything on the trunk into my backpack, loop my helmet on my arm, and head to the car.

Ember calls after me, but I don't turn to look. I'm going to go home and come back in the morning to feed my horse. Just like normal. We will be a regular family, Ember and me.

I fumble with my keys, dropping them twice through whole-body sobs. Finally, I get the car unlocked and open the backseat, but before I can get my backpack in, there's an enormous crash in the barn. I dart to the entrance and am almost trampled by Ember racing past me.

"No!" I chase after her as fast as I can. I have to stop her. She can't go tonight. *I* can't go tonight. *I'm not ready to lose her.*

Ember heads for the open pasture with the pond. I have to stop her before she gets there.

As she trots, Ember stumbles. "No," I whisper, screams no longer coming out of my tight throat.

She rightens herself and keeps trotting as smoothly as her legs can go these days. She gets to the pond as the distant church bells ring.

11:00.

Fog swirls around the pond, engulfing Ember.

"No!" I drop to my knees.

I didn't make it in time. I'm too late.

Ember is down there for the All Hallows' Eve ride and there's no turning back.

How can I keep her safe now?

7

OCTOBER 31, 2024 11:02 P.M.

My feet drag and my head hangs as I walk to the pond, avoiding looking at anyone. Ember stands close to Gigi, sitting bareback on Angelo, her sparking gray gelding. Her face is full of wrinkles that tell the story of a long life well lived. Everyone else is making their way away from the pond, but Ember, Gigi, and Angelo stay there, waiting for me.

Ember grazes near them, but not too close—she never liked Angelo—and Gigi glares at me as I approach.

"You're late," she says, unsmiling. "You aren't even mounted. Ember is running amuck. What happened? Why aren't you ready?"

Turning my back to her, I pet Ember's shoulder. She lifts her head and nuzzles me. "I'm sorry, Gigi. I…I…" I can't think of an excuse to give her that she will accept, especially with her eyes burning into the back of my head.

"We only have so much time and I prefer not to waste it if you please. Just tie up her mane and let's get going."

I nod and slide my hands over Ember's mane. My fingers braid and twist two sections together until they form a looping knot. My helmet is still on my arm, so I slip it onto my head and ask Ember to step with me towards the water's edge, where there's a big rock I can use to mount her.

Settling myself with my backpack onto Ember's delicate back, I look at Gigi. Her eyes are fixated on the full moon's reflection dancing along the clear, dark water's surface. I follow her gaze across the water from the moon's reflection to mine and Ember's. The only things reflected off the dark surface. The water is still enough that I can see my face is pale with red blotches. Ember is as beautiful as ever, standing tall and proud. She's the best horse and can never be replaced.

"Are you ready?" Gigi asks without moving her eyes from the moon's reflection.

"Yes."

She turns her horse away from the pond in one graceful motion and walks around it. She holds a knot identical to the one I just tied into Ember's mane, but she only holds it to give her hands something to do. I wish I had a bridle or at least a halter. Then I could have more control of Ember. *I can still get her out of tonight.* Somehow.

With no guidance from me, Ember follows the gray horse. I take one last look at Ember's reflection in the pond before she moves further away from the edge, making sure she doesn't slip in the mud.

Angelo splashes along the edge of the water, sometimes stepping in it, sometimes not. He and his rider are graceful, never moving a muscle out of place, perfectly in sync.

As the gray horse plays at the water's edge, Ember pins her ears at him.

"She still doesn't like Angelo then?" Gigi asks.

"I guess not. She's been good though. Just today she let the Hunter girls take pictures with her in their bright, sparkly Halloween costumes." Gigi scoffs at the idea of Halloween costumes and at the mention of the family that's living in our home. Trying to brighten the mood, I say, "She's even got used to the farrier."

"Oh?" Gigi turns around to look at me, her eyes wide.

I nod, smiling. "No more sedation needed!"

"Well now, what an improvement that is," Gigi states. "Although it can be a sign of old age. If time doesn't strengthen the fight, then it takes the fight right out—"

"I'm still working at the hotel," I cut her off. She normally asks right away about my work.

"What? The same job at the hotel?" Angelo leads us away from the pond, up through the field towards the woods to a different trail than Ember and I took earlier.

He knows our regular path well. He should after doing it for so many years. "Why? You graduated from college years ago. You're the first one in the family to have a full college education. You could really make something of yourself. You're a smart girl. There's no reason for you to still be at that job. No reason at all." Pausing for only a moment, her lips turn down and her brow furrows. "Let me guess, no boyfriend either?"

So maybe that wasn't the best distraction, but at least she's not talking about Ember and time. "No, there just isn't anyone like us. Plus, it's not 1800 anymore. I don't *need* a boyfriend."

"I don't believe there's no one like us. And I'm not *that* old." A smile plays on her lips. "You can't keep living in isolation. It's not right. You need to go out and find people. The right people."

"I wouldn't be alone if everyone would stop dying!" I don't mean to say it out loud, but I can't take it back now.

Angelo turns to face me. We're standing along the edge of the woods, ahead is the entrance to the trail. Gigi glares at me, and Ember pins her ears and stomps her feet at Angelo. "That is—"

"It's more difficult to tell who people are nowadays," I try to distract her again. I need to find a better topic where she won't be yelling at me. *Why is she just scolding me? These rides used to be the best nights of the year.* "It's not like I can just walk up to someone and say 'hey, are you a w—'"

"Shhh!" Gigi holds her hand up and looks around, finally distracted by something that's not me. The wind blows again, the dry leaves scratching against each other, falling to the ground. Gigi smiles. "I just love that sound. I miss it so much." She closes her eyes in bliss and Angelo prances to the entrance into the woods, excited for a run through the trees.

Ember starts to follow, but I sit deep in my seat to slow her. She stops in confusion and dances in place. I lean down to her ear. "Let's go back to the barn." Turning her, she won't move forward. Her ears spin in all directions, unsure of where to go.

This might be my only chance to get away tonight. *My only chance to save Ember.*

"We have to go now, Ember."

Normally I love these rides. But this year, I just can't do it. I know what will happen at the end of the ride and I just can't let it happen. Not this year.

"Dawn!" Gigi's voice is muffled by the trees.

Ember makes the decision to trot into the woods to catch up with Gigi and Angelo. And I have to just sit there and go along for the ride.

Gigi and Angelo are standing where the trail widens enough for us to ride side-by-side. She looks at the trees, oohing and aahing at the colors of the leaves.

Ember stops beside them, and we sit in silence, taking in the earthy smell of the autumn air.

Then Gigi turns her head and studies Ember's body. I feel exposed by her glare.

Ember's breathing is slightly labored from the trot, but the adventure is still in her eyes. However, Gigi looks at none of that. She looks at her legs, chewing the inside of her cheek and tilting her head. "Tell me about Ember. How has her health been?"

"Fine. Just fine. Perfect, in fact," I lie with a fake smile on my face. Gigi glares at me, and I slump forward. "She really is doing fine. She's had no big complications. She's aged gracefully. The vet is thankful for that. Vet days were always long days for all of us, but she never needed anything more than maintenance care, for the most part."

Gigi's lips are tight, but she says nothing as we walk down the path. I think back on Ember's health. She was always healthy, but feisty. Not everyone could handle her. Especially when we first met. I was only six, but I remember it like it was yesterday.

My dad took me to the local weekly auction. We were there to buy a few pigs, but because I've always loved horses, he would walk me up and down the aisle of horses to look at them. He promised he would buy me a horse of my own one day. He never said when or from where, but I studied each horse at the auction, knowing eventually I would find my horse.

On this particular day, as we were walking around, we heard an animal struggling against a chain. I ran to investigate and saw a horse tied up in a stall with a chain over her nose. I could feel her pain and panic inside of me, the pressure and pinching of the chain were on my nose as much as hers.

With one glance, I could tell she was the horse I had always dreamed about, from her red coat to her fierce personality, right down to the white crescent moon on her forehead. I knew we had been searching for each other, and today we finally found each other. I skipped into the stall, not paying any attention to the rope to keep people out, mostly because it was hanging higher than I was tall.

Putting my hands up, I started singing, "Calm my little witch, there's no need to twitch. It's time to be brave, just listen to my sound waves," copying what my mom did for me when I was scared. My hands reaching up, I finally touched her for the first time. Her anger and worry zapped into my body, but it was quickly calmed down by my cheerfulness and calmness. She immediately relaxed and I could tell she hadn't been relaxed for a long time.

"Get her out!" a man yelled. He and my dad stopped on the other side of the rope, but Ember was lowering her head, not fighting against the chain. "Well, I'll be." The cowboy took off his hat and scratched his head. "Do you know who that is?" he asked my dad.

I stood beside my red horse, humming my mom's old song to her and petting her with long, gentle strokes. She just needed someone to love her. I ran my hands down her body, releasing her tension as I went. My dad hadn't taught me this magic yet. I was just gaining control of my powers, but I knew it was working. The tension slipped off her easily with each stroke of my hand. She hadn't ever felt so good before and tried to turn her head around to give me a hug.

"Watch out! She's going to bite," the cowboy cautioned, but her ears were up, and she had a soft look in her eye. I knew she would never hurt me.

"I know exactly who that is," Dad answered his earlier question. I could hear the smile on his face. I knew he recognized the song I was humming and knew it would calm her down, just like it always calmed me down.

I took my eyes off Ember for a moment to look at the cowboy who stood outside the stall looking at me with wide eyes and his mouth hanging open. Giggling at his face, I wondered why my lovely horse was tied up with a chain.

"You're a good girl, aren't you?" I kissed her leg, the only part I could reach. "Daddy, she's coming home with us." It wasn't a question. I looked at Dad, and he nodded slightly. He knew this was my horse, too, but didn't want to make the cowboy suspicious by agreeing with me so calmly.

"I guess she is," he said.

I knew he would let me take home the right horse when I found her. This was the one I always wanted. "Yay!" I cheered and started jumping around in celebration.

"No!" the cowboy started to yell, reaching forward with his hands to stop me, but he didn't have anything to worry about. Ember stood there with her eyes closed, drifting off to sleep, her hind leg cocked.

"I'll be!" the cowboy said again, slapping his hat against his hand. "Good luck with that pair there. You'll need it." He slapped Dad on the back and walked away, laughing and shaking his head.

After my celebration, I walked right up to Ember's face. "You're coming home with us, and you're never coming back here again." She lowered her head as far as she could, and I gave her a big hug as she pulled me in close with her nose.

Waving goodbye for now, Dad and I took our seats for the auction to begin. I had to remind him to bid on the pigs we came for, but he didn't forget to bid on Ember. I was the happiest girl in the world.

It wasn't until years later that I finally understood the story from the cowboy's perspective. Ember had been in and out of the auctions around the area many times and become infamous. Ever since she was born, she had been nasty to every human that dared come close to her. Every trainer in the area had tried to handle her during her first four years, but no one could tame her. She had gained the name Fire Devil because of her color and temperament.

I was full of love from the moment my eyes laid on her. No doubts were in my head telling me to be careful or that she wasn't the horse for me. We were meant to be together, and I saw her scared and in pain. I did the most logical thing I could think of: sing to her. Dad recognized her too. I hadn't described what she looked like, but I had told him I'd dreamed about my horse.

"I played with Ember every day growing up. No one would believe that I could tame her, and I didn't, really. We just had an understanding between us. She never acted up for me or tried to hurt me."

Gigi responds with a "hmm" before I realize I was talking out loud.

"I didn't warm up to her for a long time," Gigi said. "I thought your parents were so irresponsible to let you near that horse. I swore I saw some devil in her eye."

We exit the woods, moving onto a dirt road that runs along the power lines. "That's just silly! Besides, Mom and Grandma told me stories about how you used to handle horses, and I did the same things. I even looked up some of your notes in the family book."

"Do you remember everything I've taught you?" Gigi asks, raising her eyebrows.

I almost forgot.

I was so happy to be back in my memories, being young and free with Ember, that I forgot about what I'm supposed to do tonight. We're walking away from the house and the barn, the direction I wish we were riding. They feel like they're on the other side of the world right now.

"It's time," Gigi says gently.

I close my eyes tight and look down. "No," I whisper, hoping she won't hear it, yet begging her to agree.

"Ember." Gigi's voice is soft, and she reaches out, placing her hand on my shoulder. A chill runs down my arm and I sit up straight. "It's her time. She's—"

I snap my head up to look at Gigi, a flash of anger shooting through my eyes. Her soft face turns down, and she takes her hand off my shoulder. I soften the hard look on my face.

I don't want to hurt Gigi, but how can I without hurting myself?

8

— · —

OCTOBER 31, 2024 11:38 P.M.

Gigi silently asks Angelo to trot down the road. Ember hesitates, but when I don't try to stop her, she follows. The only sounds are the soft thuds and occasional crunch of a leaf under Ember's hoof. Because of my delays, we have to hurry to make sure we get to the clearing before midnight. The place where I'm expected to say goodbye to Ember.

As we approach the bend in the road where the path leads up the hill, Angelo slows to a walk.

"Do you have the locket?" Gigi asks gently.

My hand reaches up to clench the locket under my shirt, and I nod.

I was ten when Gigi told me about connection jewelry. Mom, Dad, and Grandma all knew about it, but Gigi was the only one in the family to have such a special horse like me. She eventually accepted that Ember was staying and was a special part of my life, so she told me that when we find an animal as special to us like Ember is to me, we must forge a special piece of jewelry, just like humans that are meant to be together do. Her locket for her and Angelo sits at his grave, so that's what I decided to make. It's something that can only be done for true soulmates, two beings that are meant for each other and no one else. My parents had that connection and made their wedding rings in this way.

My dad helped me forge my locket in the fire, blacksmithing being one of his talents. The talents and hobbies my family has had over the years always amazed me. All the buildings they used besides the barn and the house haven't been entered for years, before my parents crossed over even. There's no way I can keep everything my family ever did alive. I'm struggling to keep myself going.

While pouring the liquid metal, I had to add a drop of blood from Ember and me. The blood and metal mixing popped and sizzled, sparks flying out of the mold. The smoke turned from white to red to purple back to white. An intense feeling drew me to Ember. I could feel her heart beating even though she was out in her pasture, far from the blacksmithing shed. We truly became one as the metal cooled, molding to the oval locket shape I picked out for us.

Once cooled, Dad showed me how to engrave the locket. The front has a design that's a combination of

Ember's moon-shaped mark and my birthmark, a wavy line down my thigh that looks like a wave from the ocean. Some of the engraving is faded now due to constant wear and polish, plus my skills weren't great then. The engravings came out uneven. But it's mine and Ember's locket. It binds us together forever.

Untucking it from my shirt, I look down at it, rubbing my thumb over the front. I've worn it every day. I always wanted a piece of Ember near me, especially after my parents crossed.

It is a special part of the ceremony Gigi and Ember expect me to perform tonight.

Angelo and Ember stop at the bottom of the path. Gigi says nothing, allowing me time to process.

Since it seems like I really have no choice but to do the ceremony, there's one last thing the locket needs. Out of my pocket, I take five mane hairs I got from Ember today, braid them together, and tuck them into the locket. Then snap the locket closed.

"Ready to race?" Gigi asks.

Angelo and Gigi glide into the woods at a soundless gallop, quickly disappearing into the dense trees.

Ember dances in place, eager to follow. But I'm ready to run the other way.

"I can't do this."

Ember's dance slows, and she turns her head so she can see me. Sliding off her back, we stand face-to-face. I look into her eyes. Mine must show fear and anger and a scared little girl. That's how I feel. Ember's shows gentleness. Calmness. Wiseness. Tiredness.

Readiness.

Closing my eyes, I lean into her, my hands turn into fists around her mane. Ember takes a deep breath and sighs. *"Everything will be okay."*

A calmness closes in around me and I open my eyes to Ember slowly blinking and nodding her head. I release my hands and she faces forward. After a deep breath, I look around for something to help me mount. Ember turns her head to nudge the back of my leg. I bend my left knee and jump off my right leg. She pushes me up with her face under my left leg and I land on her back, the backpack shifting at the sudden movement.

Ember faces forward again and stands perfectly still. I close my eyes. "Help me do the thing that is best for Ember." I open my eyes and lean forward ever so slightly, giving Ember permission to run.

Ember jumps into a gallop. She's never run faster in her life. She has new life again. She's young again. Maybe she doesn't have to go! We can still be together!

Ember races up the hill, gathering speed with every stride. I let go of her mane and spread my arms wide. "We're flying! We're free!"

My yells echo back to me and too soon I see the end of the path opening into the clearing. We're going so fast. *Tonight's ride is almost over for everyone but me.*

"No," I whisper and pick up her mane again, but I'm too late. Ember breaks out of the forest at top speed into the clearing. She circles the outside of the clearing, away from all the markers, slowing herself down.

I let myself get carried away. It's too late now.

9

—·—

OCTOBER 31, 2024 11:50 P.M.

Ember circles the clearing, slowing her pace. I've been here countless times before, most on this very night and time every year. It's my family's graveyard. My parents and I would often come up here, at least every full moon, to clean the graveyard and honor our family. Since they crossed, I only come up here when I need to, which is once a year.

The markers are of different varieties and form no recognizable pattern. Some are fancy carved headstones, some are just a pile of rocks, and others are wooden crosses ranging from beautifully carved to two sticks tied together. But all have some type of talisman at each marker, symbolizing the person. Some are engraved stones, some engraved leather, some jewelry, even some horseshoes. The weeds and grass have taken over the graveyard, knocking some markers down.

Gigi and Angelo stand in front of two plain but well-built crosses. The two newest in the graveyard. My parents'.

Ember stops where we first entered the clearing. Gigi's eyes are closed, so I wait quietly as she moves her hands around and whispers her spells. She does this first to my mother's grave—her granddaughter—then my father's.

"It might help if you knew the full story," Gigi says when she's finished. She opens her eyes but isn't looking at me.

I'm confused. *What more is there to know?* Five years ago, my parents abandoned me. They left me all alone for no good reason. They crossed each other over without even telling me goodbye. I don't even know how they did it. It's not possible to cross yourself over, and I've never heard of two people crossing each other at the same time.

"Your mother was sick," Gigi says.

"What are you talking about? They were both–"

"Your mother had a tumor in her brain." Angelo turns so they are both facing me. Gigi's eyes meet mine. "She was diagnosed a month before this night. She was given months to live, if that. Her time had come before anyone expected it to. And they made the decision to go together. They were special, your parents. True soulmates. Made for each other in no way I've seen or heard of before.

Nothing in this world or any other could keep them apart. They didn't want to be separated."

It can't be true. My parents loved each other like no one has ever loved before, I know that. But they were healthy. They were young. My mom couldn't have been sick. Even if she was, my dad was a nurse and he specialized in healing magic. He could have healed her. He always healed me. I once broke my arm, and he made it heal in half the time.

"If that's true, why didn't they tell me? Why did they let me watch them cross over?" Tears burn my eyes as I remember that night.

Every All Hallows' Eve, I've met with my ancestors, our family tradition. Mom introduced me to everyone in her family, but Gigi was always my favorite. Probably because she had a horse with her. Once I got Ember, we started using the hour they had in this world to go for rides while my parents talked with other ancestors. She taught me so much on those rides, about horses and magic. At the end of the hour, the family meets at the graveyard so they can all cross back to the spirit world.

That night, Gigi wasn't too eager to get back to the graveyard. I didn't understand it. We only got there right as midnight was ringing in. She was almost trapped outside of the spirit world. If she didn't go back, I wouldn't ever be able to see her again. I raced Ember to the cemetery to encourage Gigi to get there in time and got there just as my parents were doing the final step of the crossing ceremony, placing each other's wedding rings on their respective grave markers. They walked through the veil hand-in-hand and never even turned to wave goodbye.

Gigi caught up with me then. The clock had almost struck midnight. Galloping past me, she called out, "I'm sorry," as she followed them to the spirit world, and then it was over. I was alone in this world with only Ember as my family.

Angelo walks towards me. "They never meant for you to see. It was a mistake. My mistake. I—"

"You knew?" My voice breaks. "All this time? And you never told me?"

Gigi's eyes showed hurt. She's always been someone I loved and admired. She's never done anything to hurt me before. Now, she looks like I just destroyed her grave. "Dawn. It's all in the past now. We can't change the past. It's time for you to move on with your life. The first thing you have to do is to let go of Ember. You must let go of the past, of what no longer serves you, to be able to continue on into the future." Angelo moves beside Ember, allowing Gigi to reach her hand out for me to take.

"No!" I back Ember up, out of Gigi's reach. "I can't! How can I let go of Ember when I'm all alone? I understand Grandma crossing over, but my parents? No!" Never. I was eleven when Grandma crossed. She had been telling me for months that she was ready to cross, and I thought nothing of it since I could see ancestors every year.

Gigi and Angelo stay where they are. "Dawn, listen to me. It's time. You have to let Ember cross over tonight. Only then can you move forward and live your real life."

"I won't do it." I try to get Ember to move back down the path. She wants to listen to me, but she also doesn't want to leave. Her feet move franticly as she tries to figure out what to do.

Gigi speaks sharply. "You know that tonight is the night. If you want to have Ember forever, you have to let her go. *Tonight.* She can't live for another year. She knows it. And you know it. You're just being selfish and won't let her go to rest peacefully." Her eyes are full of concern and love. I know she loves me and would never ask me to do anything that isn't for my own good, but how can she know what that is anymore?

"How dare you!" Tears of frustration pour down my face. "You know nothing of my life. You know nothing of *this* life anymore. You died forty-three years ago! You were surrounded by family and friends your whole life. You never had to do anything by yourself. You never had to move out of your home because you couldn't afford it—"

"I never liked that you rented out the house." Gigi rolls her eyes.

"I had no choice!" Anger stops the tears burning my eyes. "I had a part-time job and was still in college! I had a senior horse and no one to help me. I was alone. I'm still alone." My voice catches on my words, their meaning sinking into my body.

"That's your choosing." Gigi raises her voice. "There are plenty of witches out there. If you would stop being childish—"

Ember rears up and I have to wrap my arms around her neck to keep from sliding off.

In my jumble to not fall, my eyes glance at my watch. 11:55. Three minutes till midnight.

What do I do?

10

—·—

OCTOBER 31, 2024 11:56 P.M.

I slide off Ember's back and walk to her face. I place my hands on her fine head and look her in the eyes. There is so much I want to tell her. So much I feel like I never got to. So much I need to. But I can't. My mouth is dry.

"I know." Ember already knows it all. She knows everything I have said, didn't say, or want to say.

Ember lowers her head into my body and presses in. I wrap my arms around her and hug tight. Emotions and thoughts flood into me. Her love for me, her joy at spending time together. Her love of candy canes. It all overwhelms me. Then she raises her head, forcing my hold to break.

How can I let her go now? Knowing about my parents. They didn't abandon me fully. Not on purpose. I've been so mad at them, and I've avoided seeing them the last four years. *But if Mom was sick…*why didn't they tell me? Why did Dad have to go? I have so many questions, so many *new* questions. And there's no time to ask this year. How can I survive another year with all these questions?

And without Ember.

It's not fair!

She lifts her head so her nostrils are level with my nose and blows air out and sucks air in.

Her breath and whiskers tickle my face, forcing a smile to spread on my lips.

I breathe in deeply, never wanting to forget her breath. Sweet hay. Molasses. Candy canes. It all sums up Ember perfectly.

She lowers her head to lip at the locket. *"This means everything to me."*

That's when it clicks. Keeping Ember here, it's not fair to her. She's in good health for her age, but *because* of her age, it could take a quick turn for the worse. Just today I thought I was losing her because of a stone in her foot. Do I really want to make her suffer? Can I bear to go through those thoughts for another year?

Her body has given her so much. It's given *me* so much. She's already in pain. I know it. Not bad, but it's there, constantly. Even with three rounds of healing energy today, I know there's still pain in her body, and it will only get worse. Earlier, I thought she broke her leg, an immediate death-sentence for a horse. I wouldn't ever see her again. If I cross her over now, then I can at least see her once a year and know she's forever safe. One day we will be together again.

I have to be strong for Ember. I push my parents out of my mind.

I give Ember's nose a kiss and step back, then look up at Gigi and nod slightly.

I'm ready.

As ready as I'll ever be to say goodbye to Ember.

11

—.—

OCTOBER 31, 2024 11:57 P.M.

"Tonight you will perform the crossover ceremony for the first time," Gigi tells me. Tonight is the last magic I have to learn, the most powerful. "It will secure a space in the spirit world for Ember. Her spirit will be safe forevermore. Do you have everything you need?"

I panic for a moment, before Ember nudges the backpack still on my back. I take it off and nod, slipping my helmet off and setting them both on the ground. Out of the backpack, I take the family spell book, opening it to the page marked with the black ribbon.

"Candles, herbs, satchels, ribbon, crystals." I list off the ingredients needed for the ceremony from the book. "Grave marker." Horror floods through me. I don't have a marker! I look up to my great-grandmother with wide eyes, but Ember steps over and shoves her nose in the backpack. The cross I made earlier is in there. *I don't re-*

member putting it there. "Yes, I have everything." I confirm with a catch in my voice.

"Good. This ceremony has been performed by members of our family for hundreds of years. No one can perform it on themselves, and only select animals that have touched our lives are able to partake. Only animals who have been bound to us by connection jewelry." Gigi smiles and pats Angelo on the shoulder, who lifts his head in pride. He was the last animal to cross over in our family. And there were only a few before him.

I look at Ember standing calmly beside me. "Ember is special. She taught me so much. She is a part of me. That day we first met in person, our souls were already connected. We are a part of each other."

"Animals like that are rare." Gigi smiles at me. "Now, don't forget, after crossing Ember over you must perform the family protect—"

Ring.

12

—·—

OCTOBER 31, 2024 11:59 P.M.

"It's time to start! Hurry!"

I stay frozen in place as time slows.

"Dawn, Ember's body doesn't have the strength to last another year. Tonight is the only night you can cross her over. It must be done now!"

Ember steps up to me and lowers her forehead to my chest. Calmness washes over me. *"I'm ready."* She puts her head into the backpack again and pulls out the cross.

The corners of my lips tug into a small smile, and I take it from her. She leads me to the one tree standing in the clearing and paws at the ground while looking at me.

Carrying my backpack, I join her under the tree. I cup my hand together, lifting them and opening them to the side, digging a hole without getting dirty, then set her cross at her gravesite.

Ring.

My hands pat the dirt back around the cross, securing it in the ground. I close my eyes. Then take a few deep breaths before taking the first ingredient out of my backpack.

Slowly spinning in a clockwise pattern, I mist cedar infused water around the graveyard to cleanse the space.

Ring.

Around Ember's cross, in the dirt, I draw a circle.

"Tonight, Ember will cross the veil from body to spirit."

I draw a circle in the air around Ember.

"Ember will cross from the Earth to the spirit world with the help of the four elements. Air."

The wind picks up, blowing in from the east and swirling around us. I place Mookaite Jasper, Stilbite, and Yellow Fluorite crystals on the east side of the cross.

Ring.

"Fire."

My finger draws the symbol from my locket over the black candle I took from my backpack, carving as it goes, and I set it on the south side of the cross on a bed of cinnamon, clove, and peppermint leaves. To light it, I snap my fingers.

"Water."

Seaweed and rose water are the next ingredients. I pour one jar of it into my hands and offer it to Ember. She drinks and I drip the rest onto her grave. Then pour another jar on the west side of the cross.

Ring.

"Earth."

From my backpack, I fill a satchel with apple, oak, and primrose dried herbs. Then, adding in Moss Agate, Moldavite, and Green Jade crystals, I tie it closed with a piece of green ribbon before burying it on the north side of the cross.

Ring.

"This night marks Ember's Earthly end. Tonight, I let go of my best friend. Spirit world, embrace Ember's soul, return her energy to a foal. I will see you at next year's end.

"To protect Ember on her journey, I leave our connection. This represents our love, just a section." My hands shake as they remove the locket from around my neck and place it around the cross. "I call upon you to help Ember pass through. Guide her with the best direction."

Ring.

To help her be protected, I grab another candle, a bag of crushed juniper leaves, and some oil from my backpack. I rub the oil on the candle, roll it in the leaves, and draw the family symbol on it before placing it at the base of the cross and snap my fingers.

I only now see family gathered around the graveyard. "To protect my family, a candle dressed in juniper carved with the family symbol," an open triangle pointing down with a circle in it and a line under the circle, "is lit for her at the grave."

Ring.

Ember's ceremony and extra protection is done, but I still have to cast the family protection spell. "I ask for family protection for every form. Do not protect just a selection, leave no one in a storm."

Clapping my hands over my head, twigs fly in and pile up in the center of the graveyard.

Ring.

"Spirit world, embrace my tribe. Earth world, protect all descendants. Do not take this as a bribe. I ask for everyone's independence."

I snap my fingers to start a bonfire, tossing basil and clove leaves from my backpack onto the twigs. Green smoke puffs up and is immediately swirled around by the wind.

Ring.

"I leave offerings and burn a bonfire. Air, fire, water, earth, I ask this to you, oh higher power. Please understand our worth."

The wind howls and blows in a circle around the graveyard, my hair, dust, and leaves blowing around my face. Fog appears, engulfing everything. The air is damp against my exposed skin.

I have to close my eyes. They burn from the smoke, dust, and swirling air. The spell is almost finished. I know I need to complete it, but all the energy in me just drained out, being swept away by the wind.

"I surrender and ask this of you. Please refresh this spell anew."

Ring.

"Thank you," I whisper. Gathering my strength for one final moment. I yell, "Thank you. Thank you for Ember's safe transition. Thank you for the protection of my spirit family. Thank you for the protection of my Earth family."

I spin in a counterclockwise circle.

"Air. Fire. Water. Earth. Thank you."

My eyes burst open, the air spinning around me.

"Well done, Dawn. It is complete. Now go, go build a life for yourse…" Gigi's voice fades.

Whispers come from my ancestors. I think I hear my parents, but I'm distracted by a loud whinny.

Ember's call is loud and distinct, but the wind and fog are too strong that no matter which way I look, I can't see anything.

13

NOVEMBER 1, 2024 12:00 A.M.

The final church bell chimes into the night. All Hallows' Eve has officially passed.

The wind, dust, and fog start to settle. My energy is gone and I barely control my body as it sinks to the ground.

The fires burn.

Silence and stillness surround me.

I am alone.

14

NOVEMBER 1, 2024 9:32 A.M.

My eyes open to see a pile of leaves. Pushing myself up into a sitting position, I look around. *Where am I?*

The candles have all burned out. The air is still, a faint candy cane smell lingering. I twist around in my spot, but there is no one with me.

Bowing my head into my hands resting on my knees, I want to cry, but nothing comes out. I rub my eyes with the heels of my hands, then sit up and take a deep breath.

I sit there breathing for a while meditating on last night and what it means for my future.

What *does* it mean for my future? What has changed?

Mom was sick. My parents didn't leave me for no reason. But why didn't they tell me? Why didn't they prepare me? What did they want me to do?

My back is stiff, my body aches. I yawn, the sun's rays reaching the back of my neck. I've never performed such a powerful spell before, and my memory is blank from after Ember calling out to me.

Ember. I feel like I should be panicking, but I'm not. There's a sense of calmness over me. Ember is safe. She's in the spirit world forever now. It was what she wanted. She showed me that. She was ready, but I wasn't.

I'm still not ready. I've never known life without her. For the last five years, she felt like my only connection to my parents, my magic. I moved all my magic to the barn. No one knows about my magic. No one can know I'm a witch. *No one knows me.*

I've put all my time and energy into Ember, to put off having to cross her over. I thought I could push it back forever. I never thought about anything else. *What do I do now?*

I'm still on Earth. And I'm alone. Only able to see my family and Ember one night a year. But All Hallows' Eve, when the veil is weakest and they can visit, is a full 365 days away from this moment. An eternity.

A growl grows in my throat and comes out. I smack the pile of leaves beside me, scattering them around. Some float through the air.

With a flick of my wrist, they zoom around me more, representing the tornado of thoughts rocketing through my brain. Tiring quickly, I let my hand fall and the leaves flutter to the ground. The last leaf brushes against my face, landing in my lap. I pick it up and study it. It's dry and brown. The veins sticking out, begging for hydration. I drop it beside me and give my hair a brief brush with my hands, untwisting the leaves and twigs tangled in it one by one.

Finished with my hair, I stagger up and dust the dirt and leaves off my body. My muscles are not happy with the exertions of last night. Strangely, I'm not cold from the night air or autumn ground. I feel just as warm as when I woke up in Ember's cuddle the day before.

The graveyard looks the same as it did last night. My legs protest as I collect my things scattered from my backpack.

I kneel before Ember's cross.

Leaning forward, I kiss the center of the cross and stand up, ready to leave. But I can't. My fingers reach out and carefully take the locket, putting it back around my neck. I'm not supposed to take it. It's an offering that should stay here with Ember's grave. But I can't leave it. I can't leave her just yet. Not fully.

Finally able to turn away from Ember's cross, I keep looking back at it as I walk across the graveyard until I reach the path where I felt so free last night with Ember.

The sun is high in the sky when I finally make it back to the barn. My legs objected from the beginning of the walk and are now jelly on fire. Bed is the only thing that sounds good right now. I put my backpack in my car and want to leave when the jars of water on the bench catch my eye. They hold powerful magic now and can't be left out for anyone to use, so my feet drag across the ground as I pick them up two at a time to take them into the barn.

The barn is still, quiet, lonely. I don't want to go in, but I'm pulled there with a fresh sense of energy coming over me just from walking inside. It's dark and cool, but it feels lighter than yesterday.

I secure the lids onto each jar of moon water and lock them away in the feed room. *Now I can go to bed.*

Ember's stall catches my eye. It needs cleaned. My body takes me to the pitchfork and wheelbarrow. Even with the new energy, the stall is only halfway stripped of everything when my arms feel like they weigh a million pounds. I can't leave it half done, so I power through the weakness and finish stripping the stall, dumping the wheelbarrow four times. Then I empty the water bucket and leave it beside the other one to dry.

From the feed room, I take out a spray bottle of chamomile and mist the stall in an anticlockwise circle.

It feels warmer and brighter in the barn, and although completely exhausted, I feel happier. Wrapping my arms around myself, I take a deep breath and smile. Ember's sweet scent still fills the barn.

I put the spray bottle away and see Kelly's magic mermaid shell. Picking it up, I smile weakly to myself. Childhood imagination is so sweet and innocent. If only some glitter on a shell could help. I hold it to my heart as I walk outside, deciding to leave the barn door open because it's another beautiful day. *Ember would have loved it.*

Mrs. Hunter is waiting outside for me. "Oh," I say in my surprise of seeing her.

She holds out some containers. Food and tea. Her food always makes me feel better. "Leftover chili and lavender tea," she says. "Make sure you drink the tea."

"Thank you." I take them from her and put them in the backseat of my car with my backpack and Kelly's shell.

"I. Um. Ember. She's…she's gone." I hold back tears.

Mrs. Hunter's eyes shine with tears, but her mouth stays in a warm, comforting smile. "I'm so sorry, Dawn. She was very special to you."

I nod and grab the locket. Mrs. Hunter's eyes flick to it and a frown touches her face, for only a moment, causing me to let it go.

"Please, come over for dinner anytime. We are happy to have you. And of course, like before, you are always welcome on the property. This is still your home."

"Thank you. I better be going. I'm working tonight."

She nods and walks back to the house.

I slide into the driver's seat of my car. My keys feel heavy as I lift them up to the ignition. But they turn so much easier than they did yesterday morning.

15

—·—

NOVEMBER 1, 2024 8:00 P.M.

The sky is dark as I pull into the hotel parking lot. It's one of about seven in town. After cleaning up the barn, I went home to the apartment I share with one other girl to shower, nap, and get ready for work. Sipping the tea from Mrs. Hunter on my way here helped lift my energy enough to make it through the night. I ate one thermos of her chili in my rush out the door and have the other one for a midnight snack. I didn't feel like eating, but my stomach was about to turn inside out if I didn't give it something. The mild chili helped it calm down.

My phone chimes with a text message as I take the keys out of the ignition. I haven't looked at it since Ember had her dinner last night. *That feels like a lifetime ago.* Mrs. Hunter sent a gif of a cartoon bear hugging another bear. I have no missed messages. Burying my phone in my purse, I get out of the car to walk into the hotel.

After clocking in, I chat with the daytime receptionist to find out about who checked in and who checked out and who I need to be careful about.

I greet a few people as they wander in from their nights out, but it's a very quiet evening. There's not really much to do in town anyway, even for being just big enough to not be called a small town anymore.

By 1 a.m., all the guests have left the lobby and I sit at the front desk, looking around. The other receptionist was here until eleven, but now it's just me until I get off at five. There's no housekeeping or managers around. No one is in the restaurant. There are some people cleaning up and fixing things in public spaces, and doing the laundry, but no one in the lobby. *Would anyone even notice if I leave?*

My eyes land on a painting across the lobby of a hand crushing an apple that I've seen thousands of times before but never really studied. *Why does it catch my eye now?*

"You must let go of the past, of what no longer serves you, to be able to continue on into the future." Gigi's words come back to me. The hand is holding on too hard to the apple and crushing it.

I was holding too hard onto Ember. Now that she's crossed over to the spirit world, what do I have? *A crushed apple.* I'm at the same job I've been at since high school. I have no friends. No family. No horse. I don't even live in my family's home. There is no meaning or purpose in my life. *Is this really how I want the rest of my life to go?*

Growing up, I wanted to be an interior designer. Styling homes and places people hang out. That's what I've always wanted to do. It's why I painted and repainted the barn so many times, and why I had more than one doll house. When I wasn't with Ember, I was redecorating them.

My college degree is in interior design. I graduated top of my class. All my professors said they felt like there was a touch of magic to all my designs. HA! Just because I added a positive energy crystal or sprinkled in some herbs here and there didn't mean I was cheating. A spell was almost never cast over my designs. *That* would've been cheating.

My eyes move off the painting. The chain hotel looks so generic. I've always hated it. When I'm bored on night shift, I've been known to occasionally move some things around. Minor things. Vases, lamps, pillows. Not the furniture or wall art. But those minor changes made such a drastic improvement. By the time I came for my next shift, it had all been put back. I'm surprised it's not all nailed into place.

I can't remember the last time I did that. Or sketched out a new design. *When did I forget about my dreams?*

What has happened to my life? What do I have to show for my twenty-nine years? *Nothing.* An empty barn. An empty life. I clutch my locket.

This hotel is the only job I know.

This town is all I know. It's a weird size. Big enough to not know everyone, but not so big that there's anything to do. Its biggest attraction is the college, which is, of course, where I went. My grade school was so big that I wasn't friends with everyone, but small enough I still knew everyone's name. Not that it mattered, no one really ever wanted to be my friend. And the few friends I did have moved away.

The interior design group in college was small enough I was a part of them, but still no real friends. Some of those kids graduated and went on trips around Europe, while I had to work overtime to pay farm bills, rent, and college debt. Some went to study in Asia and work at top companies in New York and LA. I mended Ember's broken paddock fences by myself.

My family became really small over just a few generations. It was once large. Cousins, aunts, uncles, and grandparents all living on the farm. But over generations, there were less kids. Then people started moving away. Gigi really hated that, but life just isn't as it used to be. Growing up, I had a few cousins who would visit with my aunt on occasion. My grandma lived with my parents and me, and my cousins mostly visited to see my grandma. My mom and her sister could only stand each other for about two days. But I haven't seen my cousins in nearly twenty years.

There were some family friends we would spend time with. They were witches too. But they all moved away. *Everyone moves away.*

I haven't spent time with a living witch since my parents. How do I find them now? It's so hard to meet people in general, but to meet people and figure out if they share your deepest secret is impossible.

"Dawn?"

I jump.

"Dawn, are you okay?" Gerry, a night maintenance man, asks.

"Yes." I let go of the locket, pick up a pen, and shuffle the papers in front of me to look busy.

"You sure? You haven't blinked for a solid minute and have been staring blankly for about five."

Genuine concern is on his face. *When was the last time someone was concerned about me?* "Sorry." I shake my head. "Just got lost in thought."

"Here, try a cherry soda. Always perks me up in the middle of these night shifts." He sets a can in front of me, raises his eyebrows, and walks away.

Once again, I am alone.

I walk into my apartment with my arms full of bags, weighed down by magazines. On my way home, I stopped at Target, Walmart, and any other place I could think of that sells magazines. I bought up every interior design magazine I could find to start doing research and find myself a job.

When I walk in, Kristen is talking on the phone on the couch, but with barely a wave, she goes to her room and shuts the door.

Time to start working on my future.

16

NOVEMBER 23, 2024 4:19 A.M.

I wake up sweating. I saw Ember. She was running through the woods, something chasing her. She was terrified and tripped, and all I could do was watch. She somersaulted and was about to roll over a cliff when I woke up.

Sleep has not been my friend lately. The first few nights after Ember crossed, I slept fine. But I guess I was so exhausted and almost asleep before I was even under the covers that no dreams would come. Since about a week after she crossed, they come every night.

There's no way I'll be able to get back to sleep. I lay here, clutching the locket. Dry eyes staring at the dark ceiling.

Some of the nightmares made me wake up screaming. Of course those happened while Kristen was here. She was at least nice enough to come check on me. We aren't really friends. I got this apartment with three other girls in college. It's two bedrooms, but the other bedroom is big enough for two beds, and with three of us splitting the rent, it was affordable.

Those two were the best of friends and seemed to only let me rent the place with them out of pity after my parents died. I didn't mind having the private room, but seeing those two always with their arms linked and whispering together definitely left me feeling left out. After graduating, they went off to Europe together, and Kristen moved in. I couldn't find two people who would mind sharing a room, so just Kristen it was. We pretty much stay out of each other's way. She's rarely even been to the apartment, as much as I can tell, for the last month. I think she said something about a boyfriend.

Rolling over in bed, I see the stack of interior design magazines in the red glow of my alarm clock. I've started applying for jobs, even internships, anything to start using my interior design degree. No one has so much as thanked me for applying. What am I supposed to do?

I'm trying to move on with my life, but someone needs to take a chance on me. Magic can't fix all my problems, but I tried casting a spell to get a new job, a spell to make my application stand out above all others, and a spell for good luck, but nothing worked.

I let out a big sigh and sit up. I've been working on design ideas, drawing sketches and even making a few models to showcase my work, but no one will look.

Getting up, I decide to sketch out some new ideas for a coffee shop before I have to get ready to go to work.

With pad and paper in hand, an antique theme comes to mind. Mismatched tables and chairs, most counters are old display cases filled with interesting things. The walls are covered with things like signs, kettles, art, and even clothes, but it doesn't look cluttered.

A few hours later, my phone chimes as I get ready for work.

We would love to have you for dinner tonight. We miss seeing you around. XX

Mrs. Hunters been nice and texting me occasionally. I've only been out there once since Ember crossed to gather ingredients for my job spells. A noncommittal reply so she knows I'm alive is the most I've responded to her, and I'm about to close the message when three dots appear.

Please come! I need your help redecorating my room! -K

I smile. Kelly wanting my help completely left my mind. She's asked me about once a year for help and has big ideas. She found some of my old doll houses set up and asked me about them. When she found out I carefully decorated them, sometimes making my own furniture or wallpaper, she begged me to help her redo her room. I refused, but Mrs. Hunter said she's helpless at decorating, especially with Kelly's big ideas, so I finally agreed. We've done ballet, cowboys, and space.

I reply, *I'll be there. Get your sketches ready.*

Tonight is going to be fun. I honestly don't remember the last time I looked forward to anything.

I clock into work and meet with the other front desk worker, Gwen, to find out what's been going on since she got here at five. It's too early for checkouts, and only a few people are up going to breakfast or the gym. I scroll through the notes on the computer for today to see how many check outs to expect. Seventeen.

"Dawn, can I see you in my office, please?" Mr. Roberts walks across the lobby looking at the papers in his hands, only looking at me and smiling after he's finished talking.

A smile plasters on my face. "Of course. Gwen, cover me?" She nods. Following my boss, we enter his office.

"Please—" he gestures to the chair in front of his desk "—sit." He sits behind the desk, scoots in, holds his hands on the desk, and smiles at me. He's not always the most personable, but he is a good boss. Doesn't put up with nonsense but is flexible when needed. "You have been one of our most loyal workers over the last twelve years. Our most dedicated young worker. It's been a long time since we've seen anyone move up the ranks like you have. You should be proud."

"Thank you?" I'm not sure what's going on or if I really should be proud of myself for that.

Twelve years? *Has it really been twelve years?* I started at seventeen, as a room attendant, then moved to hostess before being moved to the front desk.

"That's why—I'll get straight to the point—I want to offer you a promotion to manager. It has a lot more responsibilities, but of course, that comes with a pay raise and other benefits. In another ten years, you could be sitting here at my desk or even be my boss!" He chuckles. "You've done well here, and we want to help you advance your career."

I blink at his smile. A promotion? To advance my career? Is that what everyone thinks I want? A career here? When did that happen? Why did I let it happen?

My hand lifts from my lap and grabs my locket.

"Well, what do you say?" His smile fades as he studies my face. I'm guessing I look horrified.

"I…I'm not sure what to say." I avert my eyes from him, looking at my feet.

"You've worked hard and been faithful to us. You deserve it. Are you worried about not working so closely with guests? I know you value that. Rest assured—"

"I quit."

Did those words just come out of my mouth? Where did they come from? Who let them come out?

"You what?" He's frowning, and his eyes are darting back and forth.

"It's a generous offer, and I appreciate it," I blurt out, "but I don't want a career here. I want to be an interior designer. And I'm going to do that." I stand and let go of the locket. "Thank you, Mr. Roberts, for everything. But it's time I moved on and start really chasing my dream." I reach out my hand. He grabs it, frowning and looking like he's not understanding what I'm saying, and shakes it. "I'm sorry, but I have to go. I won't see you tomorrow." Smiling, I walk out of the office to the break room with employee lockers, grab my stuff, and clock out.

"Bye Gwen!" I wave as I run-walk out of the hotel. She lifts her hand with a frown and tilt of her head.

Outside, I throw my arms open, tilt my head back, and spin around.

I'm free!

17

—·—

NOVEMBER 23, 2024 8:04 A.M.

The barn is where I want to be right now, so I drive straight there and take my sketchbook, that I now carry with me all the time, inside. To get started, I get some crystals from the feed room and set them in a circle around me on the trunk. I meditate and thank the elements for helping me move forward with my life, then start sketching ideas for Kelly's new mermaid grotto.

A full sketch for Kelly's room is filled out on the page in front of me when Mrs. Hunter's voice ringing outside the barn, "Knock, knock," makes me look up. She stands in the doorway as Max runs in to greet me too. "I was worried about you being cold and hungry." She holds out a mug. "Peppermint hot chocolate. And I have lunch ready in the house."

"Oh."

Max begs for a pat on the head before I try to stand and struggle. My legs are a bit frozen in their crossed leg position. *How long have I been sitting here?* The cold now takes hold of me and I shiver.

"Thanks." The mug sends warmth immediately into my hands, traveling up my arms and down my body.

"Is that for Kelly's room?" Mrs. Hunter peaks at my sketchbook open on the trunk.

"Mmmmm," I hum, breathing in the wonderful smells and hugging the mug close to my body. "Yes, it is. What do you think?"

"Hm-hm. Yes. I think she will particularly love the ceiling mural to make her feel underwater. Gives it a mystical—" she scrunches up her face "—touch. Now, let's go eat lunch." She claps her hands and turns around. Max runs ahead of her.

Sipping the hot chocolate, I follow, leaving the sketchbook laying in the middle of the circle of crystals.

Max goes into the house first and disappears. We kick off our boots and take off our jackets as we enter, and I look around.

"Always feels strange, doesn't it?" Mrs. Hunter asks. "Seeing someone else living in your home."

I nod, still looking around in the entryway. "Have you experienced it before, Mrs. Hunter?" Even though this isn't my first visit inside while the Hunters have lived here, it always feels weird, like they have invaded my personal space.

"Not exactly," she answers, standing with me. "But whenever I go to my parent's house, I always get a feeling of that's where I really belong. That's my real home."

I look at her, wondering what she means. Her eyes are unfocused as she looks past me, then she shakes her head and meets my eyes.

"Don't get me wrong, I've loved every house I've lived in with Frank and the girls, but something about your childhood always feels the most like home. Don't you think? And please, call me Lucille."

I consider her words and slowly nod. "Yes. I think so. Until you moved in, this was the only place I ever lived. The only place I could imagine living. And I got Ember at such a young age. It's like I never knew life without her." My right hand moves from cupping the mug with my left to grip my locket.

Lucille's eyes flick to my hand and she frowns, but only for a second. "Basil tomato soup and grilled cheese for lunch. We can eat in the kitchen." She leaves me to follow her again down the small hall leading to the kitchen.

I let go of the locket as I enter the kitchen. She's already ladling soup from the big pot on the stove into two bowls.

"Have a seat. It's ready, just keeping warm. There's more hot chocolate in this pot too." She points to the smaller pot.

I hug my mug close. "I'm good for now. Thanks, Lucille. It's delicious." We smile at each other.

"Fresh peppermint and a splash of vanilla," she says, plating the sandwiches and cutting them diagonally. She carries the plates then the bowls over to the island, setting one set in front of me and the other at the next chair for her, then pours herself a mug of hot chocolate before sitting down beside me.

"Dig in."

"It looks wonderful." I pick up one half of my sandwich and bite a corner off. The bread is golden brown and buttery, and the cheese is thick and gooey. I have to use my fingers to break the cheese connecting the bite in my mouth from the rest of the sandwich. "Mmm! This is so good!" I mumble around the cheese. Then, I dive into the best soup I've ever tasted.

We eat and chat like old friends. She tells me her recipe for making the soup from scratch and about the bit of quilting she does to sell online.

After eating and starting on a second mug of peppermint hot chocolate, we both sit back, relaxing.

"Thank you, Lucille. That was the best meal I've had in a long time."

"Oh!" She waves me off. "You are very welcome, and thank you for joining me. I sometimes get lonely, always having lunch by myself when the girls are in school."

She sets down her mug and folds her hands in her lap. "Now, I don't mean to pry, but I can't help but notice you're in work clothes and you got here pretty early this morning. Is everything okay?" She raises an eyebrow but has a kind and warm look on her face that says she really wants to hear what I have to say and won't judge me for it.

"I actually quit my job. This morning." My eyes only meet hers after I say it, worried she might not approve. Maybe I made a mistake. Lucille is a proper adult. She might think it was a stupid move. My hand automatically goes to my locket, but lets it go when her eyes flick to it.

She smiles at me. "Is this what you want?"

Is it?

I nod. "I've been there since I was seventeen. I was offered a promotion this morning to advance my career, but I quit instead. I never wanted to work there long-term. I'm ready to become an interior designer, like I always wanted. I just stayed there…"

I guess I stayed there because it was comfortable. It was what I knew. But now is the time to take a chance. A real chance. Yes, I had been sending out applications, but no one was getting back to me. It's time for me to start taking action. I only have me to care for, so I can take that chance. I sat around, trying so hard to make Ember stay on Earth as long as possible, and it didn't prepare me for crossing her over. I can't do the same in my life. It's time I go and do what I want.

Lucille claps and I startle. "Yay!" She stands to give me a big hug. "I'm so proud of you."

"You are?" Surely she would think it's a terrible decision. "I don't have a job lined up yet."

She lets me go and backs up a step. "Yes, you do." I narrow my eyes at her. "In fact, I believe we owe you back pay for your previous help decorating the girls' rooms and the house."

Shaking my head, it takes a moment for what she says to register. "You don't have to–"

"Don't be silly! Of course we do. We are proud to be your first clients. Now." She picks up the plates. "Let me clean up the kitchen. You drink your hot chocolate," she scolds as I get up to help, "and we will go out to buy a few things to start on Kelly's mermaid room makeover."

18

—·—

NOVEMBER 23, 2024 7:34 P.M.

"No way!" Kelly screams, pointing to the sketch for her mermaid room. "It's so cool!" Max jumps up at her shout and barks a few times, then runs out of the dining room.

"You like it?" I smile at her.

"I love it. Hannah," she gasps, "look! The ceiling makes it all seem underwater."

Hannah looks over the sketch and smiles. "That's awesome."

"Dawn, you should help Hannah redo her room too!"

Mr. Hunter, Frank, laughs. "Your room isn't even started yet, and maybe Hannah likes her room the way it is."

"Well, I do have the time." I look at Hannah. My heart races as my eyes connect with Frank's. "I quit my job today to become an interior designer." I brace myself for a telling off.

"Congratulations," he cheers.

Kelly claps and does a happy dance where she sits. Hannah's smile brightens too.

They're all being so supportive, it's unbelievable. "I'm still looking for a job…"

"Could we do a rock concert in my room?" Hannah perks up, pushing her long dark hair out of her face. This is about the loudest I've ever heard her speak.

"That sounds like fun." My mind fills with ideas. The bed could be on a stage and we could hang up her guitars—

"We better find you a job before you redo the entire house," Frank jokes.

"Is there a mermaid looking for new décor?" Lucille sings coming from the kitchen carrying the bags with a shell pillow, bubble fairy lights, and a mermaid tail blanket we picked up today. I can't remember the last time I went shopping with anyone. Or spent that much time with someone. It was so much fun, actually. Max comes back in, too, and lies on his bed in the corner.

"I am!" Kelly raises her hands. Lucille hands her the bags and Kelly loves each piece as she pulls them out.

"And for dessert…" Lucille disappears back to the kitchen. "Mermaid cupcakes!" She carries a tray with cupcakes and glasses of milk for everyone. *When did she pick those up?*

We all cheer and eat the cupcakes, discussing ideas for Hannah's rock concert room.

19

DECEMBER 2, 2024 4:13 P.M.

Kelly's room fills with a soft blue light that shines over the walls in the same pattern as water shining in the sun. It's the final touch, and just in time. The van pulls up out front and I can hear Kelly and Hannah getting out.

"Is it ready?" Kelly asks Lucille, her voice muffled since they're outside.

Lucille laughs and opens the front door for them. "Dawn is just finishing it up now. Let's get a snack, then we can check it out. How does caviar sound?"

The front door closes. "What's that?"

"Fish eggs," Hannah tells her.

"Ewww!" I can hear Kelly's face being all scrunched up. They laugh and head into the kitchen.

They remind me of my time with my mom after school. My heart squeezes remembering those times. She was my best friend. Always. And Dad. I sit down on the edge of Kelly's bed, hold my locket, and pull my sweat-shirt into my lap, Dad's favorite Steelers one. Working to finish the room before she got home, I got hot. I'm glad that I kept it, and some of his other things and Mom's. Knowing the truth, but still not fully understanding it, I miss them so much more than I did just a few months ago.

"Dawn! Come get a snack with us," Lucille calls up the steps. My grip on my locket and sweatshirt loosens. I've spent almost all my time the last couple of weeks here. Lucille and I did the shopping for Kelly's room, and she helped me do most of the painting. Kelly and Hannah helped, too, after school. Lucille always insisted on feeding me lunch and dinner, inviting me for breakfast if I wanted to. It's like they adopted me into their family. It's nice, but strange. They aren't my family. They don't know my secret. Still, they have supported me so much since I quit the hotel. There are times, like hearing Lucille greet the girls home from school, when being around them makes me feel lonely. I miss having a relationship like that. One where I can truly be myself.

I stand, smooth out the new purple scaled comforter and take one last look around the room. Everything is just as it should be, so I head downstairs for a snack, pulling the door shut behind me.

"Hi, Dawn. We have Goldfish, not fish eggs thankfully! Is my room ready?"

Pulling out the seat at the kitchen island beside Hannah, Lucille hands me a bowl of Goldfish and I nod.

Kelly does her seated happy dance and tries to shove her whole bowl of Goldfish into her mouth at once.

"Slow down," Lucille tells her. "We aren't going up until we're all done." She picks up one Goldfish and puts it into her mouth. Her bowl looks like she hasn't eaten any yet.

Kelly grins sheepishly and carefully chews the crackers puffing out her cheeks before taking a drink to wash it down.

"I was thinking," Hannah turns to me, "maybe we could display some of my vinals on the wall in my room."

Hannah has the biggest vinyl album collection I've ever seen. Who knew they would make such a comeback? What's next, denim on denim fashion? Platform shoes? "I love that idea." We had talked about having a wall of graffiti or posters of rock stars, but this feels much more like Hannah. She even has an electric and acoustic guitar we were considering hanging on the wall. Her music taste is loud compared to her personality, so finding a good mix between the rock/pop/punk music and her soft personality has been a fun challenge.

"Hurry up! I want to see my room," Kelly encourages us. We laugh and eat our snack. Lucille asks the girls about their day at school while Kelly bounces in her seat, impatiently waiting for us to finish our snacks.

Hannah loads all our dishes into the dishwasher before Lucille says we can finally go see Kelly's new room. In her excitement, Kelly knocks down her crutches and Lucille picks them up for her. Hannah and I wait to let Kelly go up the stairs first to see her room. Having her room upstairs can be difficult with her crutches and leg braces, but she loved the house so much when they saw it and insisted they get it. And she climbs now with enthusiasm.

She stands outside her closed door waiting for us and admiring the seashell "K" hanging on it.

"Are you ready for your very own mermaid grotto?" I step up to open the door for her. She nods so hard I'm surprised she doesn't fall over. Twisting the doorknob, I push the door open and let her walk in first, followed by Hannah and Lucille.

Kelly looks around, her eyes wide and sparkling.

"What do you think?" My nerves are getting to me. Kelly's pretty much never speechless.

She circles the room, taking in every new detail.

"This is so cool," Hannah says. "Best room makeover yet." I smile at her praise.

They have already seen the walls are a blue ombré, starting at a dark blue at the bottom and going to a light blue at the top, and that the ceiling is painted light blue with the bottom of a ship. Everything else is new.

One wall has a silhouette of a mermaid painted on it. Another wall has a porthole mirror, and beside it is netting and rope with clothes pins to hang up photos and art. I put up a few photos she already had, like her and Hannah with Ember from Halloween.

A few shelves, painted the same color as the wall, are hanging up. They aren't full, but I added an old bottle with a scroll I wrote out a simple spell on and filled up some old jars with diluted moon water and added glitter to them for some real mermaid magic.

At the foot of her bed is a treasure chest. Over her bed is a light blue tool canopy.

I switched the knobs on her white dresser to be starfish. On her dresser, with her jewelry boxes, I placed the glittery shell she gave me on Halloween for Ember.

Kelly's survey stops at her dresser. She picks up the shell, and I hold my breath. *Is she mad I'm giving it back?*

A smile has yet to appear on her face as she studies the shell in her hand. Lucille and I look at each other, her face just as worried as I feel. Then Kelly looks up at me.

"I LOVE it!" She holds out her arm, inviting me into a hug that I accept. I let out a sigh of relief.

We spend a good hour looking at all the details, Kelly and Hannah saying each one is their favorite thing. All too soon, Lucille says it's time they do their homework, and she makes dinner.

We go downstairs, and I sit in the living room with the girls. I was so busy finishing up Kelly's room that I barely noticed how tired I was, but now that it's over, and she approves, exhaustion washes over me. Before I know it, I'm asleep.

20

—·—

Over the last month, I've had dinner with the Hunters more often than not, and spent a lot of time with Lucille. They've become really good friends, even if I feel like I can't be 100% me around them. Lucille is different though. She's like an aunt to me. She doesn't know I'm a witch, but I feel like I don't have to hide anything from her either.

I've been over so much working on both girls' rooms, and they have come out amazing. Kelly says she feels like a real mermaid and wants her short hair to always be wavy now. Hannah's room turned out perfect.

We got a special box to store the vinyls so she can still play them with the covers hanging on the walls. There isn't really a style or pattern to the covers she wanted to hang up, but it's her room. There's a pink cover from Melanie Martinez, a red and purple signed

Eric Hutchinson, a black and red Green Day, a yellow Radiohead, a black My Chemical Romance, and more.

Her guitars are hanging on the wall, above the amp for her electric guitar, beside her record player and an overstuffed chair for her to sit in and listen.

We didn't actually build a stage to put her bed on, but we got a red carpet to give it the feel of a stage, and along the carpet's edge and along the ceiling above it are strips of lights, adding to the stage feel.

The walls are gray with a big light up sign that she can change out the message on. Behind her bed are silhouettes of members of a band performing.

To add just a touch of magic, I added some clear crystals around the room.

They've shared pictures of their rooms with their friends and invited them over, and I've gotten several calls from parents to redo their rooms as well. I'm still applying for any interior design job I can find, but it's nice having some actual experience to show them now. Plus, Lucille handed me a wad of cash, saying it was pay for the current makeovers and the previous ones I helped with. She won't let me not accept the money, so I haven't had to worry about money yet. Which is good since I haven't gotten an interview. I've tried a few more spells, even enchanting some sketches and résumés I sent physically, but nothing.

Max comes over to me sitting in their living room and puts his big, slobbery head on my lap. It wakes me up, not that I was actually sleeping. He's a Bernese Mountain Dog. Not a breed I've heard of before, but it's not like I've spent any time learning about dog breeds. The Hunters got him right after moving in. He's a big lovebug, enjoys playing, and protects his family fiercely.

Petting his soft, black head, I ask, "What do you need, boy? Want to go out?" His ears perk up, so I unwillingly take the cozy blanket off my lap and follow Max to the front door.

The Hunters have gone away a few times before since they moved in, and they always ask me to take care of Max. They've offered to let me stay in the house before, but I never took them up on it. It was never a problem to come take care of Max when I had Ember to take care of. This time, I figured, why not? Especially now that it's not as weird going into the house since I've spent so much time here with them. And I don't know if I would be fully motivated to come over here without Ember to take care of or them to see.

At the front door, I slip on my boots, pull on my jacket, hat, and gloves, and step outside. Max doesn't really need me to be out with him, but I could use a stretch. I've been curled up on the couch all morning.

Max jumps around in the few inches of snow on the ground, and I walk in the yard, kicking it as I go. Bouncing over, Max snaps playfully at the snow I kick, so we turn it into a game. I walk kicking snow and he attacks it. I'm laughing and running with him in no time. My breath is quickly used up, and I need a breather. Looking up, I see we've made our way to the barn.

I've visited it a few more times in the last month, but it's so empty and cold without Ember. The door is shut tight against the winter, but something pulls me to open it and go in. It takes a full two minutes for my eyes to adjust to the darkness after the sun reflecting off the snow, and it feels so much colder in here than it was outside. *How is that even possible?*

Ember's halters hang on her empty stall and the trunk sits there. It looks like it always has. Unlocking the stall door, I go inside. It's empty. Seeing it this way, even though I was the one to clean it out, brings tears to my eyes. Grabbing my locket, I shiver. Ember's scent has completely faded from the stall.

"I miss you."

My nightmares have been worse the last couple of nights. I don't know if it's because I'm by myself again with the Hunters gone, or the fact that it's Christmas. I don't go a day without seeing the Hunters now. My family never did much for Christmas. We exchanged gifts because everyone else did, but mostly we rested and had a fire at the graveyard, drinking ginger tea and eating candy canes, something I started because of Ember. Sometimes we made evergreen wreaths and placed them around the graveyard.

One of our traditional gifts was a journal and pen. We'd spend the evening writing in our journals by candlelight, reflecting on the past year. When I was little, I usually just drew pictures, then I started writing about all my adventures with Ember.

The Hunters left me a few gifts and told me to wait till today to open them. Hannah got me Eric Hutchinson's *Sounds Like This* CD. She introduced me to his music, and we bonded over it while working on her room. Kelly got me a friendship bracelet kit. Lucille and Frank's gift is a beautiful new sketchbook with a galaxy pattern on the cover, and a set of really nice markers and pens. I cried when I opened it. It's not a lot, but they're the most special gifts I've gotten in a long time. Well, I haven't gotten any gifts since my parents crossed.

Standing in Ember's stall, tears streak down my face. I think about the beautiful new sketchbook and missing Ember and my parents.

Max joins me in the stall, nudging my hand for a pat. I blink my tears away from my eyes and look at him.

"Want to go on a hike?" He perks his ears and tilts his head.

In the feed room, I gather up my cedar and pine wood chips and clove, cinnamon, and frankincense. I close up the barn and call to Max. We go back to the house where I have a quick bite to eat while making ginger tea, then grab the rest of my supplies for our hike.

Huffing and puffing, Max and I finally exit the path into the graveyard. It's not the easiest of hikes, especially in the cold, but man am I out of shape. I wasn't really fit to begin with, but apparently taking care of Ember really helped a lot. I guess I should find some type of exercise to do.

Max is even tired from the hike, making his way to lie under the tree, close to Ember's cross. I stand at the entrance to the clearing, catching my breath before making my way over there too. Kneeling at her cross, I hold my locket. "Ember. I don't know what I'm doing." I kiss her cross in the center before going to the middle of the clearing.

Clapping my hands over my head causes twigs to fly through the air and pile up in front of me. With a snap of my fingers, they're on fire.

From my backpack, I pull out a tarp and set it on the ground to keep me dry, then I lay a blanket over it. Next, I sprinkle the cedar chips, pine chips, clove, cinnamon, and frankincense into the fire. The flames change color slightly with each ingredient, and I let the colors play out in full before adding the next. The clearing is warming up and has a nice, woodsy and spicy scent to it.

Perfect.

I sit down and wrap up in the blanket before pulling out a thermos of tea and my new sketchbook. Sipping the tea, I feel warm and happy. It feels like Christmas now.

Pen in hand and sketchbook open, I write the date on the top of the page, ready to journal. But my hand stops here. *What do I write?* My eyes focus on the dancing flames while I try to figure out what I should write, what I *can* write, what I *want* to write.

Max lies beside me, his warm body pressing up against my leg. I'm ready to write, and write I do.

I write about everything that happened on All Hallows' Eve. From the memories I made with Ember, to trying to leave before the ride because I didn't want to lose her, to learning the truth about my parents, and having to cross Ember over. Tears fall to the pages as I write, spreading the pen's ink into patterns, but I keep writing. Filling page after page with all my deepest thoughts, fears, and emotions I've kept buried inside.

I write about how I was so caught up in trying to not lose Ember that I actually lost myself, and in trying to find myself, I quit my job.

I write about how scared I am to actually be chasing my lifelong dream. I'm afraid I'm not good enough. I'm afraid I won't get a job, and I'll have to go back to the hotel or maybe even a worse job.

I write about not feeling so alone when I'm with Lucille, but I still have no one to share my magic with.

I fill the pages with my new hopes and dreams and fears. I fill the pages with my regrets and all the questions I have for my parents.

My hand cramps several times while I write, but it needs to come out. Everything pours out of me. All my sadness. All my loneliness. It's overwhelming and I need to let it go. Get it out of my body.

As I write, I feel lighter. My tears dry.

I close the book after my last period, and the sun is setting.

I hug the sketchbook to my chest and close my eyes. Releasing everything that was holding me back, ready to embrace the future, *my* future. I'm still sad and lonely, but not in the same way. I'm ready to move past that. I'm ready to find my life, my friends. I don't want to be alone anymore. I don't want to be sad. I'm scared to move on, but I know it's time.

The sun has fully set by the time I open my eyes. I put the sketchbook in my backpack and stagger to my feet, cold and stiff from sitting so long. Max stands up and stretches before I fold the blanket and tarp and put them in my backpack. Grabbing a stick from the fire that's only lit on one end, I snap my fingers to put out the bonfire.

"Come on, Max." Using the torch, I walk back to the path to head to the house. At the opening of the path, I turn around and look over the graveyard. I look from Gigi's grave, to my parents', to Ember's. I smile, nod to them, and turn around to take the long hike back.

21

— · —

JANUARY 31, 2025 11:00 A.M.

In the last month, I've done five bedroom makeovers for Kelly and Hannah's friends, two living rooms, and one dining room for some of their parents. Everyone says each room I touch has a sparkle to it that feels like magic. If only they knew. They have all shared pictures of my work with friends, and now I have an interview with Miss Moore.

My legs shake, and I hold my locket as I sit in the waiting room. I yawn. I'm still having nightmares about Ember. And my nerves about the interview today kept me up all night.

"Miss Medows?" I look at the secretary. "Miss Moore is ready to see you. Right through there." He points to the door on his right.

Letting go of the locket, I pick up my bag with my sketchbook and tablet full of pictures of my latest work.

My trembling hand knocks on the door.

"Come in," Miss Moore calls and I open the door. "Sit." She gestures to the chair across her desk from her.

"Hi," I say, sitting down.

"Well, this is not the normal time we hire, but I saw what you did in the Foster's house, and I can't wait to see what else you've done."

Kelly's friend Ruth asked me to do her room. And after doing Ruth's room, her parents asked me to do the whole house. So far I've only done the living room and dining room for them. Miss Moore is a friend of a friend of theirs and owns Moore Treasured Living, the biggest design business within a hundred miles.

"I'm glad you like their house." I clear my throat and reach into my bag to pull out my sketchbook and tablet. Sliding the sketchbook across the desk to Miss Morre, I boot up the tablet to show her the final pictures of my other work.

Excited to have real examples to show her, I'm self-conscious that most of them are kids' rooms. They all picked bold and colorful themes. Fun themes, but not necessarily what I want to be doing professionally. At least I have more professional designs in my sketchbook, even if I haven't been able to make them real yet.

Miss Moore flips through the sketches and pictures quickly. She's nodding but frowning as she flips.

Are they not what she wanted? They are too childish. I shouldn't have shown her the pictures. She will not take me seriously now seeing what I've been doing.

She finishes flipping through the pictures and smiles at me. "I have to say, this interview is just a formality, Dawn. I want to offer you a job."

What!? A job with Miss Moore?

"You would be my assistant, and of course your client list would become integrated with mine and you can't contract work outside of the office…"

Assistant. I won't actually be designing. That's not as exciting. But everyone has to build their way up in business. This is an amazing opportunity, especially with Miss Moore. I applied for much lower jobs with the company months ago, even an unpaid internship, and got nothing. To be handed a job like this is amazing. I really couldn't wish for anything better.

"No."

Her smile fades, and she cocks her head. "I'm sorry?"

"No." *What am I doing? Why am I declining this job? I need this job. What's wrong with me?*

"It's a very generous offer, and I thank you for it." I have no idea what I'm saying. It's all coming out on its own. "It's exactly what I've been hoping for, for months if I'm completely honest, but as you've seen, I've been doing a lot of designing lately, and I don't want to stop just to work at an excellent company. I appreciate your time today and your offer, but I have to decline." Gathering my sketchbook and tablet, I stand on steady legs and hold my unshaking hand out to her, but she doesn't take it. "Thank you, Miss Moore." I smile. I have no control over my body or mouth.

She stands, crosses her arms, and looks hard at me. "Are you sure, Dawn? This is a onetime offer. I could let you have a day to think it over."

My hand stays in the air between us. "Thank you, but no. I know what I want now. I want to do the designing."

Miss Moore sighs and shakes my hand firmly. "I don't understand, but I appreciate your confidence. I wish you luck. You are very tough, Dawn. I would have loved to have you on my team."

"Thank you." I grab my bag with both hands. "Goodbye."

She waves as I strut out of the office. The secretary is on the phone, so I walk right to the elevator. I hit the call button, it pings, and the doors open. I step inside.

What have I done?

22

JANUARY 31, 2025 11:45 A.M.

I meet Lucille at a café in the downtown area for lunch, and she's already waiting in the entryway when I walk in.

Her smile fades when she sees me. "What happened?" We were hoping this would be a celebration.

"She handed me a job, and I declined."

"You declined. Why?"

"I don't know. That's a dream place to work. And I need a job." I sigh. "I have no idea what happened." *Why did I turn down the job offer?* It's what I've been wanting. It's what I've been working towards doing the minor jobs on my own. It would have fulfilled everything I wanted. A job working with interior design. A way to make new friends. A step in my new life.

Lucille bites her bottom lip. "Why don't you sit, and I'll order for us."

I nod and walk to a table in the back.

This was the opportunity I've been waiting for. A chance to build my future, move on with my life. I'm ready to do it, so why did I decline the job?

Okay, so I wasn't actually going to be designing with this job. And I couldn't even do any designs on the side. That was a bummer, but it was also a steady paycheck. I pick up my locket and rub my thumb over it.

"There's something so much better for you."

Before I can process the message, Lucille sets two mugs down on the table and sits across from me.

"Here's some tea, and a BLT is on the way. Now, what are you thinking is your next step?" She leans in and asks it so calmly and kindly, acting like I didn't just make the biggest mistake of my life.

I take a sip of tea and cradle it with both hands. "I have no idea." My phone chimes from an incoming text.

Lucille sits back. "Check that."

I really don't want to, but I set down my mug to pull out my phone.

Hi Dawn, this is Ted Peters, a friend of the Fosters. I love what you did for them, and I want to talk to you about redoing my BnB.

"It's another friend of a friend asking about me doing work for them," I tell Lucille, setting my phone down.

"How many friends of a friend have you talked to?"

I rack my memory. "I'm not sure at this point. Half a dozen at least? And they say they're still referring me out." *What does it matter?*

She sips her tea and lifts an eyebrow. "Interesting."

I know she's thinking something but not saying it.

I replay the morning in my mind. Declining a good job with confidence. Getting asked to work on a BnB. Lucille asking how many friends of a friend I've talked to. Let's see. It has been six families in seven weeks. I've certainly been busy. All doing rooms in homes. Now I have a chance to do a BnB. A whole BnB. That's incredible. That could take months.

Wait.

I sit up straight. "I could start my own business. And work for myself?"

Lucille nods and winks.

The waiter brings over our sandwiches, putting a pause in the conversation. Lucille politely thanks him, but my mind is buzzing with ideas. Why didn't I think of this before? Can I really start my own business? What does it take? Will I fail? Will I succeed?

"You have the power within you to do it. Trust yourself. You will be great."

I can do this. I can start my own business, and it will be great! I'm almost too excited to eat now. But I still need to know Lucille's thoughts.

Leaning forward in my seat, I ask, "Do you think I can do it?" I've been doing so well getting jobs on my own and everyone has been happy with my work. It's not the traditional way into a career, but who does traditional anymore?

The sketchbook Lucille got me for Christmas and all the writing and reflecting I did in it come to mind. Ember had to push me into letting her go. She was ready, but I was scared. Is that what's happening now? I was offered a straightforward job this morning, but something made me say no. Starting my own business is scary, maybe even scarier than crossing Ember, but what do I have to lose?

Lucille takes a bite of her sandwich and chews it painfully slow before answering. "I don't see why not. Finding clients and getting referrals are some of the hardest things to get, and you have them. It'll be a lot of extra work beyond designing. Are you up for it?"

I sit back and slowly nod. "I think so. No." I look her in the eye and bang my fist on the table. "I *am* up for it."

"Good for you!" she cheers. "Eat, and we'll work on your new business."

By the time we leave, we have most of a business plan, a list of things for me to do to start my business, and a name.

Dawn's Enchanted Interiors.

23

— · —

FEBRUARY 6, 2025 9:30 A.M.

Parking outside of Mr. Peters's BnB, I hold my locket and take a deep breath. "Please let my ideas for a farmhouse make Mr. Peters as happy as a field mouse," I whisper with my eyes shut. After another deep breath, I step out of my car.

I looked the place up online. It's comfortable and charming, but a little flat. Right now, it has a modern cabin feel to it, with lots of browns and greens, leather furniture, and lots of wood. He told me he's looking to change the feel to be more of a farmhouse. He thinks it will be more warm and welcoming, plus he's had the BnB decorated as a modern cabin for a long time now.

Bits have been replaced and added that just don't fit anymore, like some light blue cushions and curtains. Not bad, but they don't mix. I have sketched some ideas and gathered some inspiration pictures to show him, but I won't know if they really work until I see the place in person and know exactly how big his budget is.

The BnB is tucked into the woods away from the noise of the town, but only five minutes outside of it. Perfect for guests. Outside looks a bit like a old cottage, with a nice big wraparound porch.

I'm admiring the porch swing when the door opens and almost hits me.

"Oh! So sorry, miss. Are you okay?" a middle-aged gentleman with salt and pepper hair asks.

"Yes," I say, a little dazed but truthfully unharmed. I was daydreaming about giving the swing a fresh coat of paint and accent cushions.

"Good. Can I offer you a coffee?" He gestures inside, and I take in the name tag on his button-up shirt and no jacket.

"Ted, as in the owner?" He nods and I hold out a newly printed business card for him. "I'm Dawn. The interior designer."

His eyes light up. "Dawn! Oh, yes. I was just coming to see if you found the place. Come in, come in!" He holds the door open and follows me inside. "You can set your stuff in the dining room where we can grab a coffee, then I can give you a tour."

I smile and follow his gestures into the room on my left, where I set my bag on the first table. I want to take some pictures of the place, so I pull out my tablet.

Mr. Peters pours two mugs of coffee. "Freshly brewed. Cream or sugar?"

"A splash of cream." I study the dining room.

"I'm scared to ask what you think so far." He hands me a mug.

My concentration face, according to Kelly, looks like "an old history teacher just sucked on a lemon." I force my lips to smile. "No, don't be. It's lovely. I like what I've seen so far. Just thinking of ideas to refresh the place."

"Ah, right to business. I like it. Shall I show you the rest?"

"Please." I sip my coffee.

He takes me to the three bedrooms upstairs first, and I snap pictures as we go. There are lots of dark browns and greens, some plaid, and art of bears and deer, but some of the key pieces, like the beds, are very simple frames that can easily be kept for the farmhouse feel.

Downstairs is a big sitting area. Comfortable seats, side tables, books, and a TV. It is open to the entryway where his check-in desk is. Behind that is his office. Then the dining room is walled off, and the kitchen is behind it. The kitchen and his office are not guest areas, so I won't be working on them, but everything else I will be.

We settle at a table in the dining room, and I show him some of my ideas and inspiration photos. We discuss what he's liking and not and talk budget.

"Keeping the old bed frames is a grand idea, maybe your best!" He winks at his joke. I know money is tight for everyone nowadays, so keeping what we can is something I love doing. Plus, so many people enjoy telling and hearing stories of how things can be repurposed. There's some other big furniture still in good condition that will match and can be kept.

"I want to keep a similar color palette, browns and greens, to what you have now. Just lighten them up so returning guests aren't completely shocked by the new look."

Nodding, he says, "I've had some people coming here since I opened it almost thirty years ago. It's been redecorated a few times, of course, but they really appreciate when something stays the same. It's a comforting place for them, and too much change won't be good. The same colors, I think, will be the perfect way to bridge them to the new theme."

I'm relieved that he doesn't hate any of my ideas. He gives me a nice budget to play with and tells me to have fun with the place. "This place needs a breath of fresh air, and I know you can do it." He holds his hand out to me. "I'm looking forward to our partnership."

I shake his hand. "Thank you so much, Ted. It's going to look wonderful!"

Ted walks me to the door. With him watching, I hold in my excitement. Once I'm down the road, well out of view, I pull my car over and do my impression of Kelly's happy dance. *I'm redecorating a whole BnB!* It's my first official job as Dawn's Enchanted Interiors.

Then I head straight home to start on new sketches and do some shopping for new furniture, art, and paint.

24

—·—

APRIL 25, 2025 4:30 P.M.

Before I started work full force on the BnB, I had a few other rooms to finish. More bedrooms for Kelly and Hannah's friends, the rest of the Foster's house, and two more living rooms. Work was keeping me so busy, I wasn't seeing Lucille or the Hunters as much, and I was starting to miss them. But then the other jobs stopped coming and I had just the BnB to focus on. It was hard work, but it's almost done. Under budget too. Ted insisted on leaving a stack of my business cards on his front desk for his guests to take. He's beyond thrilled with what I've done for him.

I have no more jobs lined up after the BnB. And the slowdown in work is nice, although I'm worried about never getting another job. Lucille says to have faith and start advertising. So far I've just gotten work by word of mouth. This weekend I'm going to brainstorm ways to advertise.

It's only in the last week I've been able to think about exercising since struggling to make it back to the house with Max on Christmas. I've taken to going to the park to walk in the afternoon. It's on my way home from the BnB, and I miss being in nature. I love interior design, but being outside is something I really need.

All the work has kept me exhausted, but my nightmares still have not gone away. Lucille and even Ted have caught me nodding off from time to time. Ted normally tells me to take the rest of the day off and that I've been working too hard. Maybe the walking and fresh air will help my sleep.

I've tried a few things to help me sleep better. Selenite and Celestite crystals under my bed and pillow, a variety of sleeping and calming spells in my family's spell book. I've put up dream catchers, tried lavender and chamomile tea. I've cleansed my room and bed countless times. Nothing works.

Pulling into the park's parking lot after working at the BnB today, I see a beat-up blue car pull in behind me. It's been here every evening this week too. It belongs to a guy, kinda cute, who also walks. We usually have earbuds in and walk alone, but today Gigi's voice is in my head. *I can't live in isolation.* Sure, I have the Hunters, but I need more than that. I need to find some other witches too. I don't really know how to, but meeting anyone new will be the first step.

He pulls in a few spots away from me and I hang out by my car, pretending to check my phone, waiting for him to get out.

"Hi," I say when he gets out and walks around to the back of his car. I clasp my hands and sorta shake them at him. He gives my hands the side-eye and I wrap them around my back. *Why did I do that?*

"Hi." His confusion turns into a bit of a smile. "I've seen you around here, haven't I?"

I smile and nod. "Want to walk together?"

He looks me up and down. "Sure."

"I'm Dawn."

"Gus."

We walk to the path.

He doesn't say anything else. *Why did I think this was a good idea?*

"Come here often?" I close my eyes. *Stupid question.* "I mean, have you been walking here long?"

"No, just a couple of months. Since I was fired."

"Oh, I'm sorry."

"It's okay. I didn't really like working on cars much anyway."

Silence.

"So you were a mechanic. That's nice."

He shrugs. "It was a job."

"What do you want to do?"

"I'm hoping a job opens up at the brewery in town."

"Oh, like a waiter?" I don't know a lot about the brewery, but I know they have a restaurant, have live music, and brew some of their own beers. I can't imagine they're fully staffed. When I was in college, everyone said they went there to hang out.

"No, I want to make the beers. What's better than that?"

He wants to make beers? "Don't you need training for that or something?"

"Maybe, but I'm sure they can train me there. How hard can it be, right? I've been practicing making wine and beers since I was fifteen."

That…doesn't sound legal. I roll my eyes. "Well, what's something else about you?"

He winks. "What do you want to know?"

He's really not helping move the conversation along. I shrug. "I don't know. Hobbies, pets, family, anything I guess."

"Hobbies: drinking beer. Pets: my roommate is a bit of a pet." He chuckles. "Family: I avoid them as much as I can."

My feet stick to the ground while he keeps walking, looking down.

"Why would you avoid your family?" If he has family around, he's so lucky. I would give anything to have my family back.

"Why should I? They never did nothing for me."

I jog to catch up with him. *His family never did anything for him?* "What do you mean? My family, small as it was, always helped everyone out."

"Dad was gone most of the time, truck driver, always on the road. When he was home, Mom and him never stopped arguing. Even if it was actually the happiest Mom ever was." He shrugs. "Neither cared about me. I was ignored until I turned eighteen and was told to pay rent or get out. So I left."

That sounds like such a horrible experience. "I'm sorry. What about grandparents or aunts and uncles?"

"Don't have none. Least, none that I know. They probably wouldn't be any better."

We walk in silence again. He offers nothing else, and I think about what he said. I can never remember my parents arguing about anything. They always said one of their favorite parts of their relationship was that the other enjoyed doing the housework the other didn't. Dad would cook, and Mom cleaned the dishes. Dad vacuumed and dusted; Mom did the laundry. Everything was split evenly between them. Except for raising me.

Dad worked more hours than Mom, but that didn't mean he wasn't around. Since he was a nurse at a hospital and his hours were always changing, Mom only had a part-time job once I was old enough to go to school. But the three of us would always go on adventures together.

They let me try out anything I wanted. We all loaded up and went to jumping shows or barrel races with Ember. They cheered from the sidelines, the pride radiating off their faces.

They also taught me magic together. They each had their skills, but even if one was taking charge of the lesson, the other would be there.

"I have to go," I blurt out. Gus is several steps ahead of me and he stops and looks at me.

"See you tomorrow?" He gives me a smile.

"Maybe." I turn around waving, knowing that I won't be back tomorrow. At least not at this time.

After running back to the car, I drive to the farm, stopping at the barn before I have dinner with the Hunters. My mind is racing with thoughts.

Since Christmas, I've been carrying around a journal with me, and now is one of those times where I *need* to write things down.

He was just creepy. He didn't look creepy, but the way he acted was so weird. I really hope I don't run into him again.

And his family. How can his family be so mean? Is that normal? I guess I know it happens, but it's so different from my family and upbringing. Is my life not normal? I mean, we're witches, of course that makes things different. My parents were happy and in love. They loved me and did everything they could to make me happy.

Or is that what Gigi was talking about? That they have "a love like no other." They're "true soulmates." Did I really have the unusual upbringing?

Gigi was right, I think. I need people around me, and the right people. Not witches necessarily. I mean, it would be great to have some witches in my life again, but they don't have to be. The Hunters prove that non-witches can be good people. I just need good people around me. Where can I find them?

25

—·—

MAY 10, 2025 10:30 A.M.

I found an outdoor summer yoga class on Saturday mornings. It's in the same park I was walking in, but being with a group should help me avoid Gus, if he comes on Saturday mornings. It also gives me exercise and a chance to connect with nature. The way it was advertised online, it sounded like it might even be run by a real witch. After the first class, I knew she wasn't. What witch would say energy can only be pulled up from the ground? Even so, it's been nice.

"Let my voice bring you back to the present moment," Tara, the yoga instructor, says. We're laying in corpse pose at the end of class. "Slowly wiggle your fingers and toes, pulling up energy into your body. As you are ready, mindfully open your eyes. Be aware of the sun overhead. And roll to one side before propping yourself back up into sukhasana, placing your hands palm down on your legs."

My eyes blink open, straining against the bright sun, and I end up rolling onto my left side with them still closed. They're able to open now, focusing on the grass beside my mat. An ant climbs up one blade just to walk back down the other side.

"Lifting your hands to your heart center"—I sit up with the rest of the class—"take this peace from today's class and let it carry with you until you're on the mat again. Namaste."

"Namaste," the class answers.

"Good class, everyone. See you next week." Tara rolls up her mat, this being her last class for the morning, and I follow her lead.

"What a load, huh?" the girl beside me whispers.

"What?"

"Carrying the peace with you. How can anyone carry any peace with them in today's world? Anyway, a few of us are going to go grab brunch over there," she nods behind me to a coffee shop. Want to join?"

I've seen her and her friends going over there after class. They don't seem like my typical group of girls. They're each in color coordinating outfits that are designer brand. Hair done perfectly. Nails manicured. Why I'm being asked to brunch I can't figure out, but why ask?

"Sure. Thanks." We roll up our mats. I give mine back to Tara, but this girl slips hers into a long, thin bag.

The other girls, with their mats in similar bags, stand with her when I come back from giving Tara the mat. "Ready?" I nod. She leads the way.

"I'm Amber. This is Ashely, and this is Anna." Amber has a big blonde bun on the top of her head and is wearing pink workout clothes. Ashley is in light blue workout clothes that look great with her dark skin. Anna is in red and has on glasses now that class is over.

"I'm Dawn." Walking across the park with them, I suddenly feel underdressed to be rolling around on the ground. I'm in sweatpants and an old t-shirt. Both stained from the barn. Ashley's long, dark hair is pulled into a neat ponytail at the base of her neck, and Anna has combed her short hair into control after posing upside down. My long wavy hair, which is usually a mess anyway, is tied in a ponytail, but I can feel pieces have fallen out. I take it out, hoping my hair being down will hide that I'm not as glamorous as them. "Have you all been taking this class long?"

"Three years." Amber seems to be their spokesperson. "The flexibility is nice to have, but Tara can be so over the top with some of that other stuff."

Ashley and Anna giggle.

"Like balancing your energy. Who can do that?" Anna pipes up.

We make it to the coffee shop, order "coffees and carbs," sit at a table outside, and chat about the class and our jobs. Well, mostly Amber talks and the rest of us listen.

I surprisingly have a good time. Although they look like the popular girls in high school, they are pretty nice. Amber insisted on buying my brunch. Ashley is a realtor and took a stack of my business cards to hand out to her clients. Anna invites me to go shopping with them this afternoon. I'm not actually sure if she's being nice or wants to help me find prettier clothes to sweat in.

"That sounds like fun, but I actually have plans this afternoon," I tell Anna.

"Do tell," Amber winks at me.

My cheeks grow red. "Nothing like that. I promised to do some baking with a friend this afternoon. A little girl. Her parents rent my family home."

"That's so sweet," Ashley says.

"If you ever want to go shopping, just let us know." Amber holds out her phone to me. "Put your number in and we can chill sometime."

I type in my phone number, thank them for the company, especially Amber, and go back to my car.

Definitely not witches either, but nice. Maybe they can help me level up my style.

26

JUNE 27, 2025 11:54 A.M.

Ashley was true to her word and handed out my business cards. I've had a few homes that are just being moved into over the last two months to decorate, and I've had more calls from friends of Kelly and Hannah's friends.

I'm now sitting in the café with Lucille, where we met after my interview with Miss Moore, waiting for lunch to arrive. My head is resting in my hand, and I watch a little girl walk by holding her mom's hand.

"Why don't you sign up for riding lessons somewhere?"

"What?" I look at Lucille. *Where is this coming from?* Her eyes are on the girl I was watching absentmindedly, and I look back at her. She's carrying a stuffed horse. *Oh.* "I don't think I can." The mother and daughter leave the café, and my eyes follow them down the sidewalk. *How did I not notice she was holding a horse?* I shake my head, trying to wake myself up.

"It could be good for you. I'm sure Ember wouldn't want you to miss out on riding without her."

Gigi told me so many stories that flood back into my mind. Angelo wasn't her first or last horse, but he was *her* horse. Angelo even seemed to be happy sometimes when Gigi told stories of her horses after him. She never loved a horse as much as Angelo, but she didn't let his crossing stop her from riding. She says she was back in the saddle the very next day on Oscar, her next horse.

But I can't ride another horse. Not until I feel like Ember has settled. My hand automatically reaches for the locket. *Not until the nightmares are gone.* It's a wonder I can function anymore with how little sleep I'm getting. I often nap during the day, but I wake up from nightmares then too.

"I'm worried about you, Dawn. You look like you haven't slept since you lost Ember." She sets her hand on the table between us. "Maybe lessons—"

"I have nightmares," I confide in her. The waiter comes over and sets down our lunch. Neither of us touch it.

"About what?"

"Ember. She's always in danger. I feel like she's not settled, and I can't ride another horse until I feel like she is." *Should I be telling her* all *of this?* I trust her. I know she won't make fun of me or anything, but I can't tell her my secret.

"So that's why you're always so tired. You've looked like you've aged years in the last six months. I've been worried about you." Her eyes drop to the locket in my hand for a moment and I let go of it. "Sometimes we need to—"

"Dawn!" Ted sees us and comes over. "How are you? She's a wonderful interior designer, you know?" He looks at Lucille.

Lucille nods. "I know first-hand how good she is."

"I've missed seeing you around since we did the BnB. Mind if I join you?"

I look at Lucille for approval before inviting him to sit down. We talk about the reactions he's gotten to the new BnB décor and how my business has been. Lucille says nothing more about my nightmares, but I know she's concerned.

After lunch, I have a meeting with another client about redoing their home. I'm not too busy anymore, but I am getting consistent work which is good. I think I'm succeeding in this entrepreneur thing.

I agreed to have dinner with the Hunters tonight, but I go early so I can stop by the barn. I'm still using it as my main hub for all things magic, even though Kristen is almost never at the apartment anymore. I'm running out of a few supplies I've been using regularly. Mainly everything I've tried to help me sleep better.

Dinner is wonderful as always, and we joke and play a board game after. Max bounces around the table as we get excited, knocking Kelly's crutches down a few times before we leave them laying on the ground.

Lucille walks me to the door as I leave, carrying a tin.

"I whipped this up this afternoon. It's a lemon verbena tea. Drink a cup an hour before you go to bed, and it should help you sleep better." Her eyebrows furrow as she hands it to me. I didn't realize my sleep could be so much of a concern for another person.

"Thanks," I say, taking the tin. I smile at Lucille, trying to reassure her. But she seems to struggle to smile back. Taking my new tea, I go home. Anything's worth a shot at this point.

27

JULY 29, 2025 7:23 P.M.

I'm having dinner with the Hunters, but the energy is off. Work has kept me away more often than I'd like, but I'm over here a few nights a week at the very least. Everyone has been quiet. Even Max lays quietly in the corner.

When they all say they're full after eating only half of what's on their plates, I can't take it. "What's going on?" My heart races.

"Dawn," Lucille starts, "we want you to know that we love you and we love your farm here, but we are moving."

"What?" I look from Lucille to Frank to Kelly to Hannah. Kelly and Hannah can't meet my eye. *Why are they moving? Is it the house? Is it me? What did I do wrong?*

Frank speaks up. "I got a job transfer. We are moving to Colorado. I start September first. We don't have all the details figured out yet. We only just found out about it."

He sighs. "We will miss you and this house. We wanted to give you as much notice as possible to let you find someone else to rent the house."

We sit in silence as I hold back tears and look at my hands in my lap. I can't believe it. *Why does everyone always leave me?*

"Dawn." Lucille places her hand on the table in front of me. "We'll keep in touch. You have become a part of this family, and nothing will take that away."

I lift my head and see her smiling. A small smile comes to my lips. "Of course. And you aren't leaving tomorrow." I try to sound cheerful. *They aren't leaving because of me. It's just life. Just like with Ember.*

"Besides," Kelly pipes in, "someone will still need to help us decorate the new house."

We laugh and spend the rest of the evening acting normal, mostly.

We serve ourselves bowls of ice cream and sit outside on the porch.

"Have you thought of taking riding lessons? I really think it will be good for you," Lucille says. Frank and the girls are catching fireflies, their ice creams melting on the porch.

Lucille's voice breaks my thoughts. I was lost in them, my gaze looking out at the barn. I look at Lucille and shake my head. "Ember meant so much to me. And…" I grab the locket and look at the floor.

"We aren't abandoning you, Dawn." I nod, not looking up. "I want to make sure you have someone, anyone, before we leave. You were so isolated before, and I don't want you to feel that way again. You need someone."

At this, I look up at her, tears sparkling in both our eyes. That's exactly what Gigi told me.

Lying in bed, I can't sleep, but I'm exhausted. Lucille's tea has helped a lot. I've gotten a few full nights of sleep. But it's not working tonight. My life was just starting to get back on track, minus the nightmares about Ember, and now the Hunters are moving. Everyone always leaves.

What's wrong with me?

I roll over and punch my pillow. The picture on my nightstand catches my eye. It's one of my favorite pictures of my parents. Knowing the truth has made me miss them on an even deeper level, so I dug this picture out of storage. I pick up the picture to look closer at it. I took it while they were playing in the autumn leaves. Ember is in the background rolling.

Why does everyone have to leave me? Why did Dad have to go with Mom?

I think back to my childhood. My parents were never apart unless one was at work. If they could, they would hold hands.

It wasn't about me though, their leaving. Mom had to go and Dad couldn't stand the idea of living without her. They spent thirty-six years together. Never spending more than twelve hours apart. Only that long because of Dad's hospital shifts.

It's how I felt about Ember. I didn't think I could live without her, that my life would be pointless. But it's not. I've built my own business, and it's successful. I'm doing what I always wanted to do, and it's even better because I have no one to answer to or please or tell me no. I thought I would be all alone without Ember, but I haven't been.

Amber, Ashley, and Anna have invited me to brunch after every yoga class. I even agreed to go shopping with them once. Anna definitely wanted me to buy some nicer clothes for yoga, but Amber and Ashley helped defend me in that I didn't need fancy clothes for yoga. They did help me get my own yoga mat and some professional clothes for meeting with clients. Not the best of friends, but it's a start.

Lucille, and the Hunters, have become my family, but now they're leaving.

I sit up. But they aren't leaving *me*. They're leaving the town because of a job. They didn't make the decision to move, and it had nothing to do with me. Frank needs a job, and this is the job he has.

Mom was sick and had to go. Dad didn't know life without her anymore.

Ember was old, and it was her time to go. I had to be the one to cross her over.

Dad loved Mom. Lucille, Kelly, and Hannah love Frank. Being together is the best thing of their lives.

Like me and Ember.

But it's different. I spent as much time with Ember as I possibly could, but it wasn't the same as the time Mom and Dad spent together. Ember is my soul mate, yes, but we are in different types of bodies. My body is meant to live longer. That means there's something else I'm supposed to do. Maybe someone else I'm supposed to meet.

I know it's not the girls from yoga, but where else can I meet people? *Maybe I should sign up for lessons somewhere.*

28

— · —

AUGUST 5, 2025 3:16 P.M.

Kelly asked me to come over and help her pack. Lucille said I didn't have to, but I wanted to spend as much time with them before the move as I can, even though it will not be goodbye. I mean, Ember and even my parents weren't really goodbye and the Hunters will be so much easier to stay connected with. I promised myself I would enjoy the time I have left with them, and then start looking for more friends.

Kelly is telling me what she's looking forward to as we pack her room when the doorbell rings.

"I got it," Hannah calls out from the living room. Max barks and scrambles after her.

Suddenly there's squealing from the doorway and I run to the top of the stairs to see Hannah hugging and being pulled around by a jumping young woman with long, wavy red hair. Max jumps around, too, not sure who to slobber on first.

"Starr! I didn't know you were coming!" Hannah says when the woman finally lets her go. They both have to push their glasses back up their noses.

"It was a surprise," Lucille calls from the kitchen. She walks out and gives Starr a big hug, then tries to calm down Max.

"Who is it?" Kelly asks, trotting out of her room. She had been wrapping things on her bed while I pack them, so it took her a minute to get up and walk over.

"Starr?" I shrug my shoulders, moving back so she can see. Hopefully she'll know who this woman is.

"Starr!" Kelly yells.

The woman looks up. "Kelly!" She runs up the stairs, two at a time, holding up her long flowing skirt. "My girl! How are you?" She scoops Kelly up in a big hug and spins her around, almost hitting me with her crutches.

"I'm perfect," Kelly laughs. "Why are you here?"

Starr looks at Lucille and Hannah. "Auntie Lucille told me you guys were moving and I couldn't believe I hadn't come to see this place for myself yet, so I had to come. I'm here to help you pack." She bows to Kelly who giggles in response.

Everyone agrees we should take a break from packing to visit with Starr since she needs a rest from her long drive. She drove from Arizona over the last week to get here.

Frank is just as surprised and happy as the girls to see Starr when he gets home from work. We spend the evening telling stories and enjoying each other's company.

29

—·—

AUGUST 9, 2025 9:30 A.M.

Starr begged to join me for my yoga class after I told her about it. She really didn't have to beg, but she started before I could tell her she's more than welcome to join.

We're sitting on our yoga mats beside each other waiting for class to start. Starr is in a romper, her hair down and wild, and her forearms are covered in bracelets. I might be embarrassed if they made noise, but she was careful to put on silent jewelry today.

"I like her," Starr nods to a girl sitting in the back by herself. She's been coming off and on since I started. Quiet. Always by herself. She doesn't always follow along with what Tara instructs us to do. Amber doesn't particularly like her.

"Why? You don't know anything about her."

Starr is in a seated forward fold, touching her toes but her knees are very bent. "Just do."

"Who's your…friend?" Amber sets her mat up behind us, Ashley and Anna following her.

"This is Starr. Starr, this is Amber, Ashely, and Anna." With her head on the ground—maybe trying to do a downward dog—Starr waves to them.

"Hiya!"

Tara steps onto her mat. "Let's get started. Sit in sukhasana, palms on the leg facing up."

Starr remains quiet for the entire class, something in it of itself special, but she is clearly not a yogi. Tara said nothing, but she gave Starr nasty looks throughout class. She attempted every pose, but they did not look great. The poses where I've always felt the most steady on my feet Starr was wobbling through. I even think I heard the girl in the back giggling at her a few times.

"Namaste." Tara ends the class, anger bubbling beneath her words.

"Namaste," the class repeats.

"That was fun! When do we meet again?" Starr asks loud enough for everyone to hear and Tara groans. She leans in and whispers to me, "Just kidding. I'll be right back." She jumps up and starts talking to the girl in the back. Starr is not shy.

I'm rolling up my yoga mat and Amber clears her throat behind me. I look at her. "We can't meet for brunch today."

"Oh?" They've invited me to join them after class every week.

They all share looks.

"Yeah, sorry. See you next time. Maybe," Amber says. They all wave and walk towards their cars. I keep my eyes on them as they walk through the parking lot and over to the coffee shop together. I roll my eyes and smile. They've been super nice and helpful, but I just don't think they're the people for me.

"Dawn." Starr skips back over, the girl from the back trailing her. "This is Esme. We have a date with her. Let's go!" She rushes me like I'm the one who hasn't put my mat away yet.

Esme tells us about a pastry shop I've heard of but never been to and we plan to meet over there. Starr rides shotgun as we follow Esme's green car onto the road.

"For someone with a yoga mat, you don't seem that great at yoga."

"Yoga isn't about the poses," Starr says. "It's about the intention. I can do the poses alright. I practice every day. I just pretended like I couldn't to gage the teacher. She's not the best."

On the short drive she tells me about some of the yoga teachers she's practiced with, and I'm amazed.

"Esme!" The couple behind the counter greet her as we walk inside together. She waves but focuses on us.

"Savory or sweet?" she asks.

"I'm normally a sweet gal, but I'm needing savory after that bitter yoga class," Starr says. I nod in agreement and Esme giggles.

"Tara is something, isn't she? The tiropitas are the best in town, the karipap is great, and the chicken pastels are filling."

Starr rubs her hands together. She seems to always be hungry. I haven't heard of any of these foods.

"Let's get one of each a split them," Starr suggests, "and maybe a banitsa with cheese and a bungeoppang too."

Esme giggles. "That's my kind of gal! Dawn?"

"Sure." Agreeing seems like the best choice right now.

Esme orders and Starr and I sit at a table. Esme brings three glasses of water.

We spend the entire afternoon sitting and chatting. Esme grew up best friends with the owners' daughter, but she moved away after college. She tells us about the paintings she does and how she's trying to sell them but works at the shop to make ends meet.

Starr tells her about her #VanLife and tea blends. Esme is impressed with some of the yoga teachers Starr tells her she's practiced with that I had never heard of.

I mostly sit and listen. Occasionally answering some of Esme's questions about me. Starr is the one to talk the most, but not in a controlling way like Amber. She makes me feel included and valued no matter how much or how little I say. It's a comfortable feeling sitting here with them. There is absolutely no judgment of any kind with these two girls.

Eventually, Lucille calls to see where Starr and I are since we promised to come help pack some more but lost track of the time. We say our goodbyes to Esme after exchanging numbers. I can't wait to hang out with her again.

30

AUGUST 17, 2025 6:23 P.M.

On their last night, Frank picked up pizzas for dinner since all their stuff was packed. He offered to take us all out to eat, but Lucille, Kelly, and Hannah wanted to spend the last evening here. We sit on the porch and eat, watching Max run around the yard.

"Well, Starr, what do you think of the town?" Lucille asks.

"I like it. I might just settle here for a while."

"Settle? I thought you liked to always be on the road," Kelly said.

Starr's van is fully set up to live in, including a small kitchen area and bed. It has no shower but a portable toilet. She drives around the country as she pleases, finding small markets to sell her tea blends at.

"I do," she tells Kelly, "but I think it might be about time to settle in one place for a bit. Open a real tea shop.

Maybe try growing my own tea even. Can't do that in a van very well."

"I think it's a good idea," Frank says, grabbing another slice of pizza. "Dawn, any new renters for this place yet?"

I shake my head. I put out a few ads, but I haven't been seriously looking. I know I could put a few spells on the ads to help them find people, but I'm not convinced I want anyone else living in my home. "With how business has been going, I think I can just about manage the bills to move back in here."

"Wonderful!" Lucille claps after setting down her drink.

"Money will still be tight for a while, but I think I can make it work."

"What about a roommate?" Lucille says, looking between Starr and me.

"Hey, yeah! Even an apartment would be roomy compared to my van, but I would feel like a queen in a castle living here with you!"

"That would be so cool," Hannah says, smiling at us.

Starr and I have gotten along really well since she got here. She's like Lucille, just a bit more eccentric. She had no problem pulling me into a hug when we were first introduced, and she's treated me like a sister ever since. She's the type of people I want to keep meeting.

"Sure," I say excitedly. "Why not? There's plenty of room, and a small rent can help cover the last of my worries."

"It's all settled then." Frank slaps his knee. "Starr moves in here with Dawn and they both run their own businesses. I feel so much better knowing Dawn won't be living here alone."

Kelly, with her mouth full, says, "They could get a dog too! And more horses."

"I'm fine with a dog or cat," Starr says. "I'm not sure about horses. They're beautiful, but they're big."

"Don't worry," Kelly says. "Dawn will teach you all about them." She gives me a big, greasy smile.

"I think starting with just a dog or cat while we build our businesses will be enough," I say, grabbing my locket. Sleep has been easier, but is still not my friend.

"I've actually been scoping out a place for sale in town for my tea shop. There's one that used to be an antique place, and a fair few things are still there and the realtor said they're going to stay there for the next owner to clear out."

"So you already looked at it. Did you put in an offer?" Lucille asks.

Starr grins sheepishly. "You know me too well, Auntie. We close in two days. Dawn, I would love for you to check out the stuff there. I want to reuse and repurpose as much as I can. It's amazing."

We laugh.

"I can't wait to see what's left! It will be a new challenge for me."

We finish our dinner and enjoy sitting outside talking. The girls take Starr to the yard to catch fireflies, and before we know it, Lucille says it's time for us to go to bed. They have a big day tomorrow.

31

AUGUST 18, 2025 9:26 A.M.

Kelly and Hannah convinced Starr and me to have a sleepover with them for their last night, so we hung out and stayed up late giggling on the living room floor. Max kept moving from one person to the next, so excited to have sleeping buddies.

My friendship bracelet kit Kelly gave me for Christmas has sat in my room unused. But tonight was the perfect time to open it.

I have a simple, sleek, black and red braided bracelet from Hannah. Kelly made me a rainbow beaded bracelet. It seemed like Starr used magic to make her bracelets. She said her technique is called macrame. She was making knots and the bracelets started twisting on themselves. It's beautiful, but I don't understand how it works. She added a star charm to each, so we never forgot who it was from.

I made braids out of yellow and red string, adding a charm for each girl that reminded me of them. Hannah got a music note. Kelly got a unicorn. Starr got a disco ball.

In the morning, Lucille woke us up, and we ate a breakfast of juice boxes and muffins before loading up the last bits into the moving truck.

"You sure you don't want help moving any of your stuff?" Frank asks when he closes the back of the moving truck once the last piece goes in. Hannah is running Max around to get his energy out.

"No. I still have some time in my apartment, so I can move it all bit by bit." I talked with Kristen, and her boyfriend, and two of his buddies are going to move in. Mine and Kristen's lease doesn't technically end until December, but we made an arrangement between the five of us for the boys to start moving in next month. Perfect for all of us.

Starr links arms with me. "And we're strong independent women, Uncle. We can manage the heavy stuff on our own."

He smiles and pulls us into a hug. "Good luck girls, and try not to get into too much trouble, eh?"

We laugh. I've never been told to stay out of trouble unless it involved Ember.

He lets us go, and Lucille comes over and whispers, "Can I talk to you for a minute?" I nod and she leads me around the side of the house, out of earshot of everyone else.

"What's up?" My heart races as I grab my locket.

"Since we're leaving, I have to tell you…" Her eyes look at my locket. The worry on her face is so concerning that I can't let go of it. "Dawn, honey, that has to go back."

"What?"

"The locket. It has to go back to Ember's grave."

"How—"

"I'm a witch. I recognized the locket right away as connection jewelry."

I'm stunned. "Are—"

"No," Lucille is calm, but serious. "Frank and the girls aren't witches. They don't know I am. I met Frank and fell in love. And decided to give up my magic to be with him. Mostly anyway." She smirks.

Her tea. Her food. She makes it all from scratch and I always feel so much better after having it. And she always made sure to feed me, especially when I was down. *How did I not see it before?* Especially with the sleeping tea. What else could have softened my nightmares? Only magic. *Powerful magic.*

"Why didn't you tell me?" There's so much I want to ask her, so much we could have talked about. It's almost like my parents all over again…

"You had to learn to be there for yourself. You've done an amazing job this year, but you need to leave the locket when you see Ember. Ember can't settle in the spirit world while you wear it."

"That's why...They're true?" My eyes grow wide thinking about the horrible nightmares and what Ember has gone through.

"I don't know how true what you've seen is, but I do know it means Ember isn't settled."

I look down at the locket in my hand. Tears sting my eyes. "I didn't know. I didn't mean to," I whisper.

Lucille pulls me into a hug. "I know! It's alright. Ember will forgive you. But you're strong enough now in yourself to not need it."

I look up at her, tears blurring my vision before they fall. "What if I'm not? I lost my parents and Ember. Now I'm losing you—"

"You are not losing me. We'll still talk, and now we can talk about everything. And you have Starr too."

Wait. "Is she a witch?"

Lucille nods. "My brother's daughter. I'm the only one to step away from magic. She does like to take some of the stereotypes pretty seriously." Lucille rolls her eyes. I think about Starr's whimsical clothing and what she's told me about her tea making and yoga experiences. "You are strong enough now, and you have people around you.

You need to leave the locket this year and start making some more friends. Starr is good at that."

I blink back tears and nod. "I will. I promise."

Lucille pulls me into a big hug and we go back to the front of the house. Kelly and Hannah wrap me up in their own hugs before they get in the car with Lucille and Max, and Frank gets in the moving truck. Starr links her arm with mine again and gives me a wink before we wave as the Hunters drive away.

32

—·—

AUGUST 22, 2025 5:16 P.M.

S tarr drives me to her new building in town. My parents and I browsed through the antique shop that was here occasionally. I can't believe how fast she committed to opening her own shop. Even after discussing how to start a business with Lucille for half a day, I was still so unsure of myself. Starr is not.

"Check this out!" She holds the door open and I step in. The space is pretty empty, but there are a lot of things piled up.

"Perfect, isn't it?" Starr shines brightly, looking over her new building.

"Is it?"

Starr grabs me by the shoulders. "Don't you see it? Here—" she runs to the right "—is the counter." She runs over to an old display cabinet. "Maybe this could be the counter. Filled with old kettles and teacups. I take your order, or I tell you your order, and over here—" she runs to the left side of the room spinning around with her arms open "—is where you sit and enjoy the tea made especially for you. A couch here." She pretends to lie down. "A table with a checkerboard here—" she mimes playing checkers "—and a shelf here full of old trinkets to be admired. Maybe even some of Esme's art around to sell."

Starr's vision is coming to life. *How did I not see it before?*

"Wait!" My shout makes Starr jump, then she comes over as I sit on the ground and pull out my sketchbook from my bag always on my shoulder. Flipping to find the right page, I ask, "Like this?" I lay the sketchbook on the ground, displaying the sketch I did for an antique themed coffee shop the morning I ended up quitting the hotel.

"It's perfect!" Starr squeals and squeezes me tight.

We jump up and start surveying what's been left behind. We move it around and find that almost everything is usable. Our biggest challenge, other than setting up the space to actually make the tea, will be to find old tea kettles and cups.

33

SEPTEMBER 13, 2025 4:06 P.M.

I'm at home searching the web for antiques for Starr's tea shop and another house I'm working on when Ted Peter's name pops up on my phone. "Hello."

"Dawn. Good to hear your voice. Let me get right to why I'm calling." He loves getting right to business.

"Not looking to redo the BnB already, I hope," I say, half joking.

He laughs. "Nothing of the sort! I've gotten so many compliments from every guest who's come since you redid it. Everyone is recommending it and I'm as busy as I've ever been. It's wonderful. I can't thank you enough."

"I'm glad to hear it." I smile.

"However, I may have an idea for thanking you. I finally convinced an old friend of mine to come for a visit after sending her some pictures of what you've done with my place. She has a few BnBs and luxury resorts of her own and would like to talk to you. She's only in town for a few days. Could you come over today?"

"Yes, I can do that. What time?"

"Now?"

"Let me gather my things and I'll head right over."

"Great! See you soon."

Well, that was unexpected.

Twenty minutes later, I pull into the BnB. I quickly take a deep breath and say a brief spell before getting out of the car. It looks so different now, with the trees starting to change colors. A couple sits on the porch swing, enjoying the day and the company. It makes my heart warm.

Stepping inside, I hear Ted in the dining room. "Hello?"

"Dawn, come in, come in. Meet Camille. Camille, this is the fantastic Dawn! Let me get you a coffee. Sit, sit." He stands to get me a coffee as Camille stands to shake my hand before I sit beside her.

"Dawn, so nice to meet you." Her French accent surprises and delights me. "I love what you've done here. It's been so long since it was up to my standards." She winks. "That's why I didn't visit before."

194

Ted sets down my coffee. "Don't listen to her. She was just scared of my manly magnitude." He winks at me, and Camille and I roll our eyes. Not because Ted isn't a man, but because he's very happily married.

"Dawn, show her the Fosters' place, and that idea you have for a coffee shop," Ted encourages.

I pull up pictures of my previous work on my tablet to show Camille before we look through my sketches.

"I'm actually using this antique coffee shop sketch for my friend's new tea shop."

"It's wonderful. You have a very wide style, Dawn."

"Thank you."

"I have a BnB in London. It's one of my one-offs, and I would like you to do it."

Me? Work in London? I stare at her wide-eyed, knowing I have to say something but am too stunned.

"That sounds great, doesn't it, Dawn?" Ted prompts me, nudging my arm with his elbow.

"Yes. Sorry. I mean. I'm speechless. Me? Really?"

Camille laughs a sweet laugh. "Yes really. If you want to. Not everyone wants to travel for work and I understand. But I must confess, I am still looking for someone to redecorate my luxury resorts all over Europe. If I like your work in my London BnB, the job could be yours."

Europe? "Yes. I would love to go to London!" I've never even traveled out of state. Going to Europe sounds amazing! Is this my future?

"Good, good. I will, of course, pay for your travel to London, provide you with a place to stay, and give you an allowance for food on top of your salary. I will have my secretary get the contract ready and send it to you. Once the London BnB is done, we'll talk more about my resorts in Paris, Greece, Rome…" she waves her hand as she lists these amazing cities. "But I have other designers to meet before I decide who to give that contract to." She smiles sweetly, her eyes scrunching up so they almost disappear behind the thick black liner and lashes. "If you'll excuse me—" she looks at her watch "—I'm so sorry, but I have another meeting. It was so nice meeting with you, and my people will be in touch."

"Of course." I gather my stuff into my bag. "Thank you so much for seeing me. I look forward to talking more." We shake hands and Ted sees me to the front door.

"Thank you so much! That was amazing!"

"Do as good a job for her as you did for me, and you'll be drowning in jobs around the world." He winks.

I slip out the door dreaming of traveling the world when Miss Moore walks up the front steps. She looks up and spots me. "Dawn, hello."

"Hi." I'm not sure how to interact with her. I don't want to be rude, but I imagine I left her with a bit of a sour taste in her mouth. And it appears we are competing for the same job now.

"Seeing Madam Camille about the resorts, too, I take it?" She eyes up my bag. "I've heard you've been doing quite well for yourself this year." She gives me a warm smile. "Congratulations. Now, if you please excuse me, I have a meeting. Nice seeing you."

I step to the side to let her pass. "Thank you. Good luck."

She nods as she walks past.

I let out a sigh of relief and whisper, "Thank you." I'm glad that wasn't too awkward.

34

Starr's tea shop had its grand opening last week. The interior turned out so cool, everyone loves it, almost as much as Starr's tea. I invited Ted to the grand opening, and he's been telling all his guests about it. Esme's paintings are displayed there, and a few have sold already.

Starr makes all her own tea blends, getting her supplies from small farms around the country. We've been scoping out some places around the farm where she can start growing her own. She decided to not plant anything until spring, but next year, using our combined knowledge and magic, we can keep her plants going year-round.

She infuses her tea with magic, just like Lucille did, and she likes to talk to her customers to figure out what type of magic they need and give them their order based on that.

The way Starr can infuse her teas is completely new magic to me, and I love it. She's been making me Lucille's sleeping tea and I'm sleeping better. Still have nightmares, but I think the universe knows I'm going to put the locket back where it belongs, so it's giving Ember and me a break.

I sit in the living room with my nighttime tea and open the new interior magazine I got today. Starr sits beside me with her own cup. "Tell me about Ember."

"I've told you everything." Starr and I have stayed up late sharing our life stories with each other. She feels like the sister I never had.

"Your connection. Really tell me about your connection." Holding her mug in her left hand, her thumb spins a ring on her right. She wears a lot of jewelry, and other than her eyebrow piercing, this ring is the only piece she doesn't change out.

"We were two souls meant to be together. I dreamed about her before meeting her, and she refused to be with anyone besides me. She was my best friend, besides my parents. I didn't want to ever let her go. But that's not life I guess."

Starr is quiet. "Life is not fair." She plays with her ring and stares into space.

I flip through my magazine, knowing Starr can really get lost in thoughts.

After about ten minutes, she asks, "Do you have any of her mane or tail hairs left?"

"I think so. Why?"

"Go get them."

Sipping my tea before putting it and my magazine on the table, I go to my room in search of the hairs. I've learned it's best to not question Starr sometimes and just do as she asks.

Finding the hairs in Gigi's old jewelry box, I take the box downstairs.

Starr drinks the last of her tea and takes the box.

I pick up my tea to sip as I watch her.

She picks out the hairs carefully, one at a time, checking their length and setting them into three piles. Once she's sorted enough, she picks up a few hairs from each pile, each section a different length, hands me the end where they're all even, and starts braiding them. As the short strands come to their end, she picks up some medium hairs to add to it. She repeats this until it's about six inches long.

"Right or left?"

"Left."

She takes the mug out of my left hand, sets it on the table, then pinches the braid below my fingers. She circles the braid around my wrist and starts braiding it onto itself. She keeps braiding and adding hairs as needed until it's a thick, strong rope around my wrist.

"Cement these hairs together so that Dawn can have her spark forever."

The bracelet glows red and Starr lets it go. The glow fades and I hold my arm up to study the braid. Ember's hair, shades of red with a few white and black hairs mixed in. It's solid. No beginning. No end.

"Now you can put the locket back without giving up all physical connections to her." Starr looks at the bracelet. She smiles, but sadness is in her eyes.

I squeeze her hand in mine. "Thank you."

35

—·—

OCTOBER 31 10:59 P.M.

I 've been sitting at the pond since sunset. I can't wait to see Ember!

Starr sat with me for a while, but being from Georgia originally, she found it much too cold.

My eyes move between my watch and the pond. *It's almost time.*

Mist starts to come off the pond's surface, spinning around. The wind picks up, turning the mist into a fog that's hard to see through. I stand at the water's edge and take a few steps back. Fog and mist swirl around in the air and it feels like I'm going to be picked up and swept away by it. My arms guard my eyes. Then I hear her.

Ember calls and I look around. She's running out of the mist and fog right to me. I open my arms to greet her and throw them around her neck when she gets near. She pulls me in close under her neck with her head. I couldn't be happier. The coldness of her body takes my breath away for a moment, but once I'm able to take a deep breath, candy cane and molasses and sweet hay fill my nose. *Ember.*

"Oh Ember! I've missed you so much."

"Hello to you, too, dear," Gigi says from atop Angelo as they approach.

"Hi Gigi!" I smile at her and look around. My ancestors are coming out of the fog and walking through the field. "Where are Mom and Dad?"

"They'll meet us at the graveyard later. Mount up and let's ride."

I take Ember over to the rock I used last year to mount her. Oh, what a year it's been!

Once mounted, we start our ride going around the pond and Ember feels like she's floating over the ground. I glance across the dark smooth surface of the pond and see only myself reflected back.

"Tell me, how has the year been? You look much happier than last year, but tired. Are you sleeping well?" Gigi studies me.

"It's been a wonderful year, Gigi." As we ride into the field and through the woods I tell her everything from quitting my job and starting my own business to talking to the guy at the park, and lastly about Lucille and Starr and Esme.

Starr, Esme, and I have been doing yoga together at the farm. They take turns leading since I'm still learning, but it's been wonderful. Starr told me she was sure Esme was a witch when she first saw her, but now realizes she's not. It's okay though. She's an amazing friend.

Gigi, me, and our horses spend our time enjoying the fallen leaves on the trail, Ember pouncing on them like she loves to do. Gigi and I swish our hands to get as many leaves piled up on the trail for her to play in.

Ember still keeps her distance from Angelo. *Some things never change.*

Ember and I move in perfect harmony like she can read my mind. She doesn't step one foot out of place.

"So you're back to living in the house then, with Starr, who's also a witch," Gigi confirms as we start down the road. I nod. "Good."

All too soon, we're looking at the path leading up to the graveyard. I ask Ember to stop, and my smile fades for the first time on the ride.

"What's wrong, dear?" Gigi asks.

Without taking my eyes off the path, I respond, "Nothing. I was just thinking about last year. I didn't think I could let Ember go. She was my everything. It was the hardest thing I ever had to do."

I lean down and wrap my arms around Ember's neck. "This year it feels so different. I'm so different." I sit back up.

"I've missed Ember every day, of course, but I wouldn't have had today if I hadn't let her go last year. I wouldn't have had anything in my life today." Images of my last year flash through my mind. The hotel. Miss Moore. Lucille. Ted. Starr. Esme. *I'm a completely different person.*

"I'm where I'm meant to be. That was the path I was supposed to follow. I wasn't living like I was meant to last year. This year I am." I smile at Gigi. She returns it.

"Race you to the top?"

"You're on!" I laugh.

Ember and Angelo take off galloping up the trail in perfect harmony. We laugh, letting our arms float out to the side, and I enjoy the feeling of complete freedom and safety.

36

OCTOBER 31, 2025 11:57 P.M.

Gigi and I break out of the woods and into the graveyard at the same time. Ember circles it one way and Angelo circles it the other as they slow from their floating gallops down to a walk.

My smile couldn't be bigger as I run my hands up and down Ember's mane.

Gigi gasps, looking around the graveyard. "What happened here?"

"I thought it needed some extra love. I've been neglecting it over the years." I lower my head in shame. "But I hope this can make up for that. I won't let it go again."

"It's beautiful," a familiar voice says behind me. I turn to see my dad leading my mom out of the darkness of the woods, holding hands.

"Dad. Mom." I can't believe my eyes. I slide off Ember's back and run to them for hugs. I cry into their shoulders as they hold me tight in their icy embrace.

"You have done so well for yourself this year. We are so proud of you," Mom whispers in my ear with a catch in her voice.

"I'm sorry for everything. I understand now though, why you did everything like you did. I was mad for a long time, but I'm not now. You two were the best parents. Thank you for everything."

"We're sorry we didn't tell you. We knew we should have, but there are just no words to tell your little girl that you're leaving her alone," Dad says. "We never meant to hurt you. We were cowards."

"I know you didn't, now. It's actually so beautiful to think about. And look who I've become." I open my arms and stand taller. "I'm who I was always meant to be, and I couldn't have been it without *everything* you have done."

Ring.

The smile on my face fades and time slows. I want more time. I've only just gotten my parents back.

Dad hugs me. Mom hugs me. "We're so proud of you. You are an amazing woman. We couldn't want anything more for you. We'll see you next year." They wave.

Ring.

Ember nudges my back. Tears blur my vision as I gently squeeze her head. "I'm sorry, Ember. I'm so sorry I took the locket." I take it off and we walk to her cross. Hanging it back up, it lines up perfectly with the middle of the cross, where the two twigs connect and are tied together with Ember's mane. It will stay safe here forevermore. Just like the talismans of my ancestors' past. Ember bows her head, closes her eyes, and sighs. "I love you."

She pushes her head into my chest. *"I forgive you."*

"Is it okay if I start riding other horses?" She nods her head, jumping into a small rear. I guess that's a yes!

Ring.

"I love you all!" Everyone is coming into the graveyard now.

I pick up the basket I left earlier, full of everything I need for tonight, and take a deep, soothing breath.

Ring.

Circling the graveyard in a clockwise pattern, I spray cedar infused water.

Ring.

"Air. Fire. Water. Earth." I turn to the east, south, west, and north as I speak to each element. "Help these spirits cross back to their world so that they may venture over to this one next year."

A candle dressed in juniper and carved with the family symbol is already at everyone's grave. I snap my fingers twice to light them at the same time. "Tonight, I burn candles for each of my ancestors."

Ring.

I walk to the center of the graveyard. "I ask for family protection for every form. Do not protect just a selection, leave no one in a storm."

Over my head, I clap, and twigs pile in front of me.

Ring.

"Spirit world embrace my tribe. Earth world protect all descendants. Do not take this as a bribe, I ask for everyone's independence."

A snap of my fingers ignites the bonfire. Into it, I toss basil and clove leaves.

Ring.

"I leave offerings and burn a bonfire. Air, fire, water, earth, I ask this to you, oh higher power. Please understand our worth."

From the basket, I take out a jar with a potion in it to pour onto the bonfire as an offering. The fire glows brighter, and the flame shoots up into the air.

Ring.

The wind swirls around the graveyard. Mist swirls in and leaves spin in the air. "I surrender and ask this of you, please refresh this spell anew."

Ring.

"Thank you," I whisper, my energy fading. "Thank you," I yell, wanting to give this spell my all. "Thank you for Ember's safe transition. Thank you for the protection of my Spirit family. Thank you for the protection of my Earth family."

I spin in a counterclockwise circle.

"Air. Fire. Water. Earth. Thank you."

With the spell finished, I turn to wave and watch my whole family walk into the fog.

Ring.

Mom, Dad, and Gigi wave to me. Angelo nods his head. They turn and walk back to the spirit world. Safe for another year.

Ring.

Ember is the last to go. She calls out and throws a buck before turning to gallop and join them. Her call resonates out in the air longer than the last chime of the bell.

My arm aches as I wave until the wind dies and everything settles. In front of Ember's cross again, I close my eyes, a smile on my face. I settle on the ground to meditate while the candles and bonfire burn down.

Once the last candle has burned out, I slowly stand and use the basket to collect the remnants of each candle. I follow the reverse path as when I placed them, ending at Ember's cross. Kneeling, I give the locket a kiss. Then stand and leave without looking back. I walk confidently back to my new life, excited about what tomorrow will bring.

Stay Connected

Dawn and Starr have told me they want more books! Sign up to my email newsletter to be first to know when their stories come out and get writing and editing tips.

Join my email list at **pxl.to/legup/subscribe**
Find all my links at **LegUpBookEditing.com/Links**
Follow me on Instagram: **@LegUpBookEditing**
Follow me on Facebook: **Leg Up Book Editing**
Email me: **bloemker.joyce@gmail.com**
Read my blog: **LegUpBookEditing.com/Blog**

EDITING SERVICES

Are you a writer?
Check out my developmental and line editing services at
LegUpBookediting.com/Editing

I offer free sample edits on 1,500 words.
Email me at **bloemker.joyce@gmail.com** to learn
more.

ACKNOWLEDGEMENTS

Wow. I'm writing the acknowledgments to my first book. I can't believe it!

Thank you first to my parents. You have always supported my dreams and addictions. Without your help, I wouldn't be publishing my first book. Thank you both for all the support over the last thirty years.

Thank you to my brother for being a good brother, helping start my book addiction while I was still in the crib, and helping me with my website.

Thank you to Michaela and Lauren for being my best friends, encouraging me, and always being there when I need to vent.

Thank you to my amazing friends who supported and believed in me as I worked on this book. Thank you Dawn, Stacy, Bonnie, Janine, Tom, Kim, Sarah, Caitlin, and Rock.

Thank you Becca Own for loving this story and helping me shape it from the very beginning.

Thank you to my editor, Morgan Waddle. I'm forever grateful for your extrovertedness that swept all us introverted editors together at EFACon 2023 where we met. I've enjoyed keeping in touch and getting to work together. I knew when I was reading your sample edit and literally laughed out loud and said "I would've said this same thing exactly like Morgan did," I knew I found the perfect editor for Ember's Cross. Thank you for working with me and helping calm me down during my few freak-outs.

Thank you to my equestrian author friends for encouraging me and offering help. Including Tiffany Noelle Chacon, Sarah Hickner, Heather Wallace, Jenny Roman, Sally O'Dwyer, Chelsey Burris, M. J. Evans, Kathy Simmers, and Anna Sochocky.

Thank you to all my online equestrian friends, including Denise Alvarez and Cathy Woods.

A special thank you to Susan Friedland, an equestrian author and teacher of the Aspiring Author Jumpstart. Without the Aspiring Author Jumpstart course, I would not be publishing my first book right now! (And maybe not for ten years!)

Thank you to my may editor friends who encouraged me on this journey including Jen Tolnay, Amy Carbo, Em Syth, Linda Ruggeri, Brittany Dowdle,

Tara Whitaker, PollyAne Nichols, Cara Walker, and Katharine Schmidt.

Thank you to my many beta readers who gave me some great feedback that doubled the word count.

Thank you to Boo Boo and Trinity, my horses. I know there were weeks when I didn't get to see you two as much as we all would've liked, but without you I wouldn't have had any of the inspiration for this book.

Thank you, readers, for giving my debut book a chance! I hope you enjoyed this story. Dawn and Starr have told me they have more to tell!

ABOUT THE AUTHOR

Horses and reading have always been Joyce Bloemker's favorite ways to spend time, and as she grew up writing joined the herd. When she isn't spending time with her horses, she is either writing or reading about them. As her writing progressed and she worked towards her BA in Creative Writing and English, Joyce discovered she has a passion and talent for editing. Joyce has been editing fiction books since 2022 and decided 2024 was her year to publish her first book. Joyce has big plans for her writing career next including more stories from Dawn, stories from Starr, and some nonfiction books.

www.ingramcontent.com/pod-product-compliance
Lightning Source LLC
Chambersburg PA
CBHW032035310726
48972CB00002B/686